10197

No Bed of Roses

BOOKS BY FAITH BALDWIN

No Bed of Roses

*

FAITH BALDWIN

Holt, Rinehart and Winston
New York   Chicago
San Francisco

Library of Congress Cataloging in Publication Data

Cuthrell, Faith (Baldwin) 1893–
No bed of roses.

PZ3.C973No [PS3505.U97]   813'.5'2   72-91591
ISBN 0-03-007681-1

FIRST EDITION

Designer: Andrea Clark
Printed in the United States of America

This book is dedicated with affection to Dr. Howard B. Gotlieb, who, for some obscure reason, removed me from what Macaulay has called "the dust and silence of the upper shelf"

Marriage is like life in this—that it is a field of battle, and not a bed of roses.

—ROBERT LOUIS STEVENSON

No Bed of Roses

1

✱✱✱✱ Young Mrs. Palmer, one midafternoon in early October, was engaged in driving a prospective client from the more rural reaches of Little Oxford to the railway station. This was the second time she had taken Mrs. Emerich to look at the old Grantson place; but on the first occasion Mrs. Emerich, a pretty, vivacious woman who talked in italics, had been accompanied by her husband, a man who said very little, mostly in discouraging negatives.

"It's all so *beautiful*," Mrs. Emerich remarked for the tenth time. "It must be fabulous in the spring—all those dogwoods."

"I've lived here four years," Katie Palmer said smiling, "and all seasons are lovely."

Privately, she thought, I could do without winter, however enchanting it looks when it's not snowing, sleeting, raining or blowing.

Mrs. Emerich sighed. She said, "Eric can be so *stubborn* . . . but you know how *men* are." Katie knew; she often reflected upon male stubbornness. "I showed him the photographs you sent me . . . the property in summer and spring; the one with snow on the fields and trees, and that *darling* little frozen brook." She sighed. "He wasn't impressed. He said even in snapshots *he* could see the need for extensive repairs."

"I hope Mr. Emerich will change his mind," Katie said, meaning it, "and realize that the advantages outweigh the disadvantages."

"I'll work on him," Mrs. Emerich promised. "My heart's *set* on the place. It isn't as though he had to go to the office every day. Anyway the commuting is good, and we wouldn't be too far from the village. I've even spoken to our help about it—asked if they would be willing to come with us or not? I was prepared to plead, even to *bribe*. The cook's a treasure; her husband's almost as good. They've worked in the country before—and liked it. I told them about the shops, the movie house, their church and all, and of course we'd give them a car. Winnie—that's the upstairs girl and parlor maid—the heavy cleaning is provided for. . . . There are cleaning teams here, aren't there?"

"Lots of them," Katie assured her.

"And perhaps you could find me another Winnie, a native?"

Katie said she could try. The agency often found domestic help—live in or out—gardeners, baby sitters.

Mrs. Emerich laughed. They wouldn't require baby sitters she said unnecessarily, as Katie knew there were no children by this marriage—and the two by Mr. Emerich's first were both grown and married. "Well," Mrs. Emerich added, "maybe, if the grand kids come and we all want to go out. . . ." She added that she understood the social life in Little Oxford was exciting. "We know the Howards slightly," she said. "They live on Cherry Lane. It was through them that we came to you."

Katie said, yes, she understood that the agency had sold the Cherry Lane house before she herself had come to the area.

Driving through the main street, which was Colonial Way, Mrs. Emerich exclaimed, as she had on her previous tour, over the shops, the trees, the quaintness, and added that she loved people, *adored* giving parties, and was *mad* about the country.

At the depot, Katie miraculously found a parking space, opened the car door for Mrs. Emerich and walked with her to the platform. She remained there, listening, until the train came in, and Mrs. Emerich boarded it, crying, "Thanks a million. You've been *wonderful*. I'll call you in a day or two."

The train pulled out toward the city and Katie returned to her car. A couple of taxi drivers who had also unloaded passengers spoke to her and she answered, calling each by name. Then she drove out of the station and a moment later turned right up Parsons Hill where she bore right again for the village parking lot. Cars came whizzing out and she avoided them with an adroitness born of practice. There were several vacant spaces. She edged into one, put a coin in the meter and walked back to the Hill, dodging a car or two. Walking briskly downhill she encountered Si Wescott toiling up. She thought: He really should lose about twenty pounds. But then, his wife's such a good cook, a treasure, she thought further, smiling, thinking of Mrs. Emerich.

"Hi, Katie," said Wescott, stopping, "you're looking gorgeous as usual. How's business?"

"Thanks. It's not exactly gorgeous," she told him. "It picked up last spring and summer, and is fair to middling now. Which of course you know very well, but winter's another matter."

"Things are getting better," she said optimistically. "How's the Bosslady?"

"Hitting on all eight."

"I didn't know there were eight of you," Si remarked, pleased with his little joke.

He was the publisher-owner of the Oxford *Weekly Beacon*, a paper read by everyone in the village and by many in areas outside Little Oxford. The *Beacon* was a good weekly. It had excellent coverage of the activities social and otherwise of Little Oxford and of some of the smaller towns nearby. It covered local sports and the schools, spoke out on zoning and local politics, printed letters to the editor and pictures of area disasters—fires, floods, wind damage—club meetings, church news, and drew steady advertising revenue from Little Oxford and much of the area beyond. Engagements and marriages, promotions of local citizens, many of whom commuted to the city—horse shows, dog shows—you name it, you'd find it—but very little scandal, unless it was something of national interest.

"How about Jeremy? Haven't seen him lately."

Si saw a lot of people; he had a competent editor, good reporters and an excellent photographer. He belonged to a good many organizations, and had no intention of retiring for a long time. He could now take it a little easier, enjoy his wife's cooking, his grown children, young grandchildren, his community status, and very comfortable home.

"Jeremy," Katie said obediently, "is fine—and very busy."

"Glad to hear it," Si said, looking pained. Jeremy Palmer took little or no interest in what went on around him and while he belonged to various community organizations, he rarely attended the meetings.

Katie reflected, having parted from Si, that was a Chamber of Commerce gambit. Jeremy had never belonged to any group in the city, unless it had to do with books. The fact that he did so now, in what was loosely termed the country, was due to the urging of friends and relatives. She laughed aloud, remembering Si's facial expression. Jeremy didn't advertise the bookshop in the *Beacon*. The shop had been there on Colonial Way for a very long time before—almost four years ago—Jeremy had bought it, lock, stock and barrel and assumed the long, costly lease.

Now she turned the corner of Parsons Hill and Colonial Way where the office in which she worked was third from the corner, ground floor. On the window: Warner and Associates, Realtors. The names of the associates were not given.

She thought: If only I could sell the Grantson property. Wow! It had been on the market for over two years, and the Grantsons had moved back to the city. No one had been able to sell it. Working on commission, thought Katie gloomily—a feast today, a famine tomorrow—which wasn't entirely accurate. The Grantsons' asking price was high. They'd come down, of course, but even so, jam on the bread and butter.

Katie went into the reception room and raised a dark, inquiring eyebrow at Flo, the harried young woman who received visitors, buzzed intercom and handled the telephone —except Mrs. Warner's; she had a private wire.

Flo nodded. "Any luck?" she asked.

"I don't know—yet. She's in then? . . . Is she alone?"

"Expecting you. She's buzzed me twice." The telephone rang and Flo answered. "Warner and Associates. . . . I'm sorry, Mr. Wilcox is out. Shall I have him call you when he comes in?"

Katie knocked at the Bosslady's door and was bidden enter. Mrs. Warner occupied—in what was known as the command post—a large chair behind a neat, formidable desk. She was a neat, formidable woman: tall, heavy, her tailored dress without adornment, her thick gray hair untouched by stylists. She had—and now displayed—a warm smile, but her large blue eyes, which were far-sighted, were cool. She said, "Katie, I expected you sooner."

"Mrs. Emerich wanted to go through the house again," Katie told her, "also walk in the fields, and into the woods. . . . My feet hurt."

Mrs. Warner rose, went to a filing cabinet, pulled out a folder and remarked, as if in accusation, "Over two years!"

Katie wished she could take off her shoes, but if she did, she'd never get them on again. She said, "Well, it's such a barn of a house—ghastly to heat—and Joe—that's the caretaker, who lives there—doesn't do much around the place. The grass gets cut, the leaks are fixed . . ." She shrugged. "But Mrs. Emerich's in love with it. First time I showed it to her, Mr. Emerich was with her. I didn't have to tell him about the roof, the cellar, the pipes or the furnace. I didn't have to tell him about anything. Nothing escaped him. But she's on her way to New York now, to persuade him that if she can't have it—and an army of plumbers, electricians, heating and termite experts, landscape gardeners, painters, plasterers and interior decorators—she will absolutely collapse. Put the last three words in quotes."

"And?" inquired Mrs. Warner, returning to her mahogany fortress.

"She's to telephone—if she succeeds."

Mrs. Warner said, "I've known the Grantson place for years. It could be made beautiful and comfortable if the money's there. Also, the land's very valuable now and the value will increase. It's one of the few sizable properties left."

"I know, and she does, too."

"Any bets?"

"Ten to one . . . a quarter—no, make it a buck—on Mrs. Emerich," Katie ventured, smiling brilliantly and Mrs. Warner thought, as she often did, that it is both interesting and unusual to find a natural blonde with dark brown eyes.

"What makes you so sure?"

"I'm not. Whoever is, in this business? But she must be at least twenty years younger than Mr. Emerich."

"Speaking of properties," Mrs. Warner said, "I think we have buyers for the Warren Andrews house—interesting people, from New York. He's just retired. They're visiting the Richards here and were taken past the property. Tim Richards called me—I'm showing it myself tomorrow . . . and I'll get hold of Warren Andrews tonight. He's been bugging me ever since the Folsoms left—you remember, they rented it? Andrews is in Nice, or Paris . . . he keeps me informed of his whereabouts. . . . I'm sorry, Katie. I know how you feel about that house. If only you'd been able to talk Jeremy into buying . . ."

"No way," said Katie, and rose. "I'm sorry, too." Disappointment was an obstacle in her throat. She tried to swallow it.

Well, Jeremy wasn't twenty years her senior and she wasn't Mrs. Emerich.

"I've a couple of things to do before I go home. See you . . ." she said, and left for the cubicle with her name on the door to make some notes and to dig into files.

Emily Warner looked at the door closing behind the straight young back. Katie had been with her only four years, but she was an asset. Clients liked her; she had inborn social graces; she worked her head off, was persuasive, but not aggressive and Emily wondered, as she had for the past two years, why Katie had married the tall quiet man—oh, granted that he was attractive—who, lived in and for books.

Well, why did anyone marry anyone? she thought, and raised her chilly blue eyes to the photograph on the wall opposite. Why, for instance, did I marry Bob? She knew why and she answered herself honestly: Because no one else ever asked me.

Emily had met Bob Warner at a house party out on the island. He had been born in Little Oxford, and she, some twenty miles away from it. He had been, at that time, a kind, bumbling young man, with a small real estate business. He was honest and inefficient. After their next few encounters on home grounds, Emily had taken an enormous interest in real estate; she had also learned all she could about it and before their marriage equipped herself to become his partner.

Bob Warner had died a good many years ago, comparatively young, from emotional malnutrition, people said.

Now Emily spoke to Flo on the intercom. "Where's Wilcox?" she demanded.

"He just called in; he'll be here in half an hour. There have been two calls for him."

Emily selected her associates with care. Carl Wilcox had been with her longest. He was a wispy wistful-looking man of indeterminate age. He lived wisely, well, and alone. He was always to be found as the extra man in the best houses. And he evoked the maternal instinct in elderly women, also in middle-aged females whose sons had married the wrong girls. Therefore, he had special success with clients who fell into these categories, and many did.

Emily had lost an associate now and then, to death, marriage or restlessness. Now there was Wilcox; two fortyish, reliable, nice and willing women—one divorced, the other a widow—and Katie, youngest and most recent, who had come to Little Oxford from an upstate city after two years in her uncle's agency. She had taken the right courses and read the right books and Emily had chosen her for her appearance, eagerness to work, and personality.

In recent years, Emily rarely went into the field with prospective clients; she'd served her time at that . . . she'd spent a lot of years selling. Now she personally took on only those who were friends and would have no one else, people who were extremely difficult—she wondered if she shouldn't have a crack at Mr. Emerich, but decided against it—or fantastically rich. The couple to whom she would show the Andrews place were at any rate rich enough to buy it at the asking price.

For the most part she was content to plan and suggest strategy to her associates, slave drive, cajole, guide, inspire, reprimand and regard. She was over sixty. She could retire. She had all—or almost all—the money she needed to keep her in solitary comfort, maintain the elegant little saltbox in which her husband had been born; hire help, give occasional lavish parties, take cruises when business was slow in winter, and buy the most expensive dinner and cocktail frocks in Little Oxford or any other town for that matter, few of which became her.

Emily liked Katie. If she'd had a daughter—she'd never had time—she would have liked her to have been rather like Katie Palmer. She did not favor her among the associates; she favored none above another. But she wished Katie had been able to have the Andrews house; Jeremy could have swung it, she thought.

Jeremy must have cashed in on the old brownstone in New York, which he had sold before coming to Little Oxford. After the Palmers' marriage, Emily had asked Katie about it casually. But, if Katie knew, she wasn't telling. She'd simply said, "Jeremy's father was lucky . . . he had the bookshop with the two upstairs apartments. He and his wife and, of course, Jeremy lived there. I suspect Jeremy cut his teeth on rare editions if no one was watching. Mr. Palmer bought the building during the depression, and remodeled the apartments for more living space. At the time he and Mrs. Palmer were killed in the plane crash and Jeremy had inherited it, the entire block was slated for demolishment and modern buildings . . . so Jeremy sold, of course."

It didn't stand to reason that Katie wouldn't know what price he'd received. In any case, Emily would wager the proceeds of the Andrews sale—of which she was almost certain—that Jeremy Palmer had a considerable sum in investments and cash. Yes, he could have swung the Andrews deal. She'd asked Katie once why he hadn't "seeing your heart was set on it."

Katie had said, "He wasn't interested in comparative antiquity, air conditioning, a swimming pool and a patio. He just wanted to rent for a while, within walking distance of the shop and then added, "He's put a lot into the shop."

So he had, Emily had admitted . . . air conditioning, there, and renovations; and he'd kept those of his predecessor's staff who chose to remain, and added others.

2

✳✳✳✳ Katie retrieved her car from the parking lot, there were still some minutes left on the meter—be grateful for small favors, she thought—drove out the back way and over to Holden Avenue. The traffic was comparatively light. Holden Avenue and all the streets leading into or out of it were lined with big maples, and the houses, set back from the road, were surrounded by trees, dogwoods, maples, burning bushes and here and there a mountain ash.

Autumn swept annually through Little Oxford like prairie fire, setting it ablaze, or descended upon the trees and bushes like an outpouring of many casks of full-bodied wine, intoxicating to sight and spirit. The season had not yet reached its height and even after the glory had peaked and passed, there would still be color under graying skies, the tenacious oaks clinging to their rosy, brown leaves until springtime came again.

Normally, since childhood, the valiant decline of the year had brought Katie wonder and delight. Earlier today she had looked and ached with beauty as Mrs. Emerich exclaimed driving to and from the Grantson place, walking in the woods, or leaning on old stone walls, marking the dangerous brilliance of poison ivy, the crimson, poison sumac, and the innocent woodbine. But now, driving home, she was indifferent and preoccupied.

She was not given to receiving telepathic communications but ever since she'd left the office she'd thought, with Emily: Jeremy could have swung it.

She loved him and had, from possibly the first time she saw him, when Warner Associates, as the agents for the bookshop building engineered the transfer of the lease from the bookshop's lessee, Mr. Purdy, to Jeremy Palmer . . . or, if not then, the second time, when she'd been asked to the Gordon Banks' house for dinner. Jessica Banks was a second cousin of Jeremy's mother. He'd been staying with the Bankses and, as Katie told Jeremy afterward, Jessica probably said, "We'll have to have a girl for Jeremy. He's met most of them by now, so it should be someone young, new, refreshing." And so she had thought of Katie, whom she'd known only through her occasional church attendance since her arrival in Little Oxford.

Katie had long since decided that she didn't understand Jeremy wholly nor he, her. She'd said so upon occasion; she had a low boiling point and he often angered or exasperated her. The first time he'd said evenly, "That's par for the course," and swung her into his arms. "Who wants total understanding? I'm sure it's wrecked more marriages than the lack of it. Admit you're never bored!"

No, she was never bored.

Now she anchored her thoughts on a hot bath and the preparation of dinner. She was not a good cook. She'd learned the basics in her mother's kitchen, but recipes— whether in books, on radio, TV, or whispered from friend to friend—had never turned her on. During her first two years in Little Oxford she'd shared a small apartment in a dull, sunless brick building with the friend who had persuaded her to come here and look for a job. During that period Katie had been forced to exercise what culinary knowledge she had. She and Linda took turns and Linda had said more than once, "I like my own cooking better, but I also like someone else to do the work and the dishes." Anyway, in that period she and Linda often went out on dates, double or single.

She thought: I must call Linda.

Linda had married shortly before Katie. They'd been friends in college, and kept up with each other even after Katie had left and Linda stayed on. Now Linda and her husband lived in the nearby town in which both had grown up. They'd been engaged when Katie first knew Linda; they'd broken it off about the time Katie had to go home to work after her father's death, and during the time she and Linda lived together, it was on again, off again with Tom. "Too silly," Linda had said after one violent quarrel. "Girls only marry the boys next door in books."

But eventually she had.

The Palmers lived on a short street off Holden Avenue. There were only six houses on it. The place they'd rented was half of a two-family house, a large, elderly structure, so remodeled that each had half a front porch, a back porch, also divided, and two entrances.

Katie left the car on the street and walked around to the back. She disliked wedging the car into the garage they shared with the Elders, as their side also contained bicycles, paint cans, odds and ends. Jeremy always put the car away when he came home.

The house, which was owned by Si Wescott, was kept in excellent repair. Each half house had a basement, an oil burner and also a small attic. Jeremy had yelped in anguish when Katie took him to see it and told him the rent. Firmly she pointed out the advantages: back from the rather narrow road, a big yard space running into woods, and, as he'd specified, within walking distance of his shop and her office. Yes, of course they paid for their utilities, including heat, but the road was plowed by the town and all Jeremy had to do was clear his front and back steps, and his part of the sidewalk.

"All!" said Jeremy gloomily.

But he'd been amused when she found—and not through her own office—the house on Baker Street. He was a Sherlock Holmes buff and spent large sums on his own collection of first editions, limited editions, illustrated editions and also on the innumerable books written about the Baker Street immortal. Privately Katie thought he looked rather like Sherlock—tall, lean, and a little stooped; also he smoked a pipe. He did not however indulge in drugs, or play a musical instrument or wear a deerstalker cap and—what was it Sherlock wore?—an Inverness? Anyway—a cape. And it was Katie who said occasionally, "Elementary," adding however, "my dear Holmes!"

As she walked around to the back she almost fell over Lancelot, who was sitting on her steps. He was a large dog of indeterminate breed, always friendly and hungry and he belonged to the Elders and their teenage boys. Katie bent to ruffle his heavy uncombed coat and said, with resignation, "One of these days I'm going to break my neck, you fool dog," and let herself in the back door which opened into an adequate kitchen, beyond it the dining area of the big living room. "No fireplace," Katie had told Jeremy sadly when she took him to see it and he'd said, "I never liked hauling logs or coals and ashes."

Off the living room there was a small study, which Jeremy had equipped with his father's desk and chair and a number of bookcases. The Elders used their similar room as a spare bedroom.

Stairs led up from the small entrance hall to the big bedroom, bath, and a smaller bedroom. Off Katie and Jeremy's bedroom was a sun deck looking into the woods and reached by glass doors. They often had breakfast, sometimes even supper on the sun deck. Jeremy cheerfully brought up trays. Sometimes they ate on the back porch, evenings, if the mosquitoes and the Elder boys were busy elsewhere. They were a highly articulate team—twins, and devoted to hard rock and roll. No one had told them it had died or was dying.

The Elders were good, untidy neighbors, young, despite their name. Olive Elder was given to screaming at the boys or Lancelot and to popping in for coffee if Katie happened to be home. She liked discussing her married life with girlfriends. The people who had lived here prior to Katie and Jeremy were, Olive said, "Older than God and snootier. Deaf too. They had stereo and played it full blast. Classical stuff. The boys nearly went nuts."

Frank Elder was a salesman and a good one. He was away a great deal, which was something of a drawback, for when Olive tired of TV or the boys' stereo afflicted her, she'd just run next door with a plate of very good cookies. Jeremy enjoyed her. He liked people, all kinds of people and Katie never knew whom he might bring home. Once she said irritated, "If you like people so much, maybe you should be writing books instead of selling them."

"Maybe I should," he conceded, smiling, "but I can sell other people's books, Katie."

She was halfway upstairs when the telephone rang and

she ran the rest of the way to take it on the bedroom extension. Jeremy had inquired, "Why an extension? We don't need it," and she'd replied, "I do. Mrs. Warner and sometimes clients often phone me late at night."

"Good God!" Jeremy had exclaimed, shocked to the core.

Linda Davis was on the other end of the wire and Katie said, "I'd every intention of calling you. How are things?"

Linda said, "Wonderful. Tom got a raise at the bank and I'm pregnant. So come over Sunday, you and Jeremy, and we'll celebrate."

They talked for ten minutes and then Katie said, "See you at six, Sunday. I have to run now. Jeremy will starve if I don't."

"He will anyway," Linda predicted.

Katie looked at the bedside clock. Hot bath, then take the chops out of the freezing compartment. When she thought of the price of a couple of bags of meat and groceries—no, she wouldn't think about it.

She ran her bath and crawled in; hot, hot water and perfumed bubbles. She wiggled her toes, lay back and almost fell asleep. Jeremy never got home before six and often later. Something was nagging at her, a psychic pain. The Warren Andrews house. She thought: Maybe those rich, wretched people won't buy it. But what good would that do? she reflected further. Jeremy wouldn't buy it if he owned all the oil in Saudi Arabia.

Reluctantly, she left the tub, wrapped herself in a voluminous terry-cloth robe, put her feet into terry-cloth slippers and went downstairs to get out the chops. So little for so much. If she were like Linda, she could take the most commonplace and inexpensive items and turn them into gourmet meals, nourishing too; Tom had to watch his weight.

Katie went back upstairs to get dry and dressed. From

16

the clothes closet she selected a floor-length hostess gown in soft yellows and browns. It had been a Christmas gift from the Bankses and Jeremy liked it. From her modest jewel case she chose the topaz necklace and earrings he'd given her at the time of their marriage. Thus fortified against small lamb chops and what went with them, and having brushed her hair and reddened her mouth, she descended to the kitchen. By the time she heard Jeremy arrive and put away the car, the table was set at the end of the living room, the salad made, the main ingredients of their drinks assembled, and she was ready to cope with chops, hashed browns, string beans, cheesecake—all conveniently frozen—and coffee.

Jeremy came in the back door, announcing unnecessarily, "I'm home." He kissed her, remarking, "You're beautiful. What's for dinner? Never mind, my distance vision is excellent. . . . I thought of calling you and suggesting I take you out, but deduced you'd be doing KP. Besides we're going to Jessica's tomorrow night and the next—Friday isn't it?—we're being taken to that absurdly expensive French place in Saltmarsh."

"Who's taking us? . . . That's where Mrs. Warner feeds her super-special clients."

"Don't you ever call her Emily?"

"No. You do, but I wouldn't dare. I got out glasses for drinks—Scotch for you, vermouth for me. Will you get the ice and water and bartend?"

"Don't I always? We'll imbibe in the study."

You haven't told me about Friday night, Jeremy."

"It's a long story. Contain yourself, woman."

He picked up a tray with the glasses, bottles and napkins, put ice in a bowl, took bottled water from the refrigerator, and, whistling, vanished.

Katie warmed the plates, and marshaled her forces. She'd

have time for a drink before she served. Then she went into the study.

All the furniture in the half house was Jeremy's. In the study, in addition to his father's desk and chair, there was a small old love seat, two other comfortable chairs and an antique game table, and on the wall space not taken up by bookshelves there were a couple of prints and photographs of his parents.

Katie came in. "You forgot the coasters and cheese crackers. I've brought them."

"So I did. Sit down here, beside me." He handed her her drink. "To us," he said.

She drank obediently. "Friday night?" she asked in a small voice.

"Oh, that. . . . You've often heard me speak of Ross Cameron?"

"The man who was in the service with you?"

"That's right. He called me this afternoon. He's driving up Friday to stay at the Village Inn and look for a house he'd like to buy."

"A house!" She sat up straight and nearly spilled her drink.

"That's right. Told him you'd help him."

"Has he a family?"

"One little girl. He's divorced. The mother has custody."

"Then he won't need a big house," said Katie, thinking: There's another prospect for the Grantson place if Mr. Emerich says no.

"Big enough to do some entertaining. Ross swings."

Katie asked, "What's he do and why is he coming here?"

"I've told you before. His father is senior partner in a big —and even today—prosperous brokerage firm. Ross is a young vice president and as to why he wants to buy in

Little Oxford, he said he once had friends here and liked it; also he can commute—car or train."

Katie, nibbling on a cracker, asked thoughtfully, "Money?"

"More than enough, despite alimony, which I understand embraces an unreasonable amount. His ex-wife has plenty of her own. He wrote me at the time of the divorce . . . Now and then he calls. I've told you about him a thousand times, but this is the first time you've shown any interest. I saw your beady little eyes glisten when I mentioned he wanted a house."

"Beady little eyes!" She pinched him hard on the thigh; he put down his glass, kissed her, and said, "If you make this sale, I expect to share the commission."

Katie wasn't listening. "The Warren Andrews house would be perfect for a swinging bachelor," she said.

"Perhaps," Jeremy agreed after a minute. "Your dream house, and you'd even get asked there. I didn't like it, but then I was biased because you wanted it and I didn't."

Katie said mournfully, "Mrs. Warren's showing it tomorrow, but if it doesn't sell . . . then Saturday I could take your old buddy there."

"Okay. I promise nothing, but Ross was always susceptible to young female charm. . . . Isn't it time we ate?"

Katie fled to the kitchen, and presently they were at the table, and he said thoughtfully, "Maybe you're improving, or perhaps I'm just hungry."

"I bought you an extra chop."

"Splendid. Tomorrow night, at Jessica's, we'll eat like princes and Friday like kings."

"Sunday," said his wife, "we're going to Linda's and Tom's. It's a celebration. He's had a raise, and she's pregnant."

"I," said Jeremy, "shall never get a raise. All I do is give them. And you don't want to be pregnant."

"Elementary," she began and he said, laughing, "that's the right word, pregnancy being elementary."

Katie brought the extra chop and waited while he had that and also seconds on the beans. "Anything unusual happen today?" she asked.

"Just Cam's call. . . . People came in to order Christmas cards. They've been doing it since August. I don't know how I'd get along without Mary Hawes."

Mrs. Hawes did the buying of greeting cards, stationery, small gifts, gift paper, bright ribbons and wool. These were items which Jeremy's father had not stocked. He had offered current books, fiction and nonfiction, but not what he called tripe. He sold, and found for buyers, books which were out of print; and offered old, valuable books, also books in other languages, first editions, and he bought for collectors. It was on the plane trip—to buy at auction a book much wanted by such a collector—that he and his wife had died.

"She's good," said Katie of Mary Hawes. "How's the new gal working out?"

Jeremy had recently hired a young widow who had come home to live with her parents. He was shorthanded as some of the older employees had retired. He'd need extra help at Christmas, too. Some of the women in the shop worked only part time, year round, save for vacations. And there was always a turnover in the college help. Boys who did errands and worked in the stock room.

"Beth's fine," he said. "She had some library experience before and after her marriage, remember?"

"She won't last long," Katie predicted.

"Why not? She seems to like the work."

"Too good-looking, I understand," said Katie, "and you do have male customers."

"Most of them married," her husband reminded her, "or of retirement age."

"You'll see," Katie said.

They cleared away companionably, Katie washed and Jeremy dried. She said, "Go smoke your pipe somewhere. I'll finish up. Did you have enough to eat?"

"Took the edge off," Jeremy admitted. He was always hungry and never gained a pound. "But I'll make up for it, tomorrow, Friday and Sunday."

"It's too bad that when I lived with Linda some of her skill didn't rub off on me."

Jeremy passed her, slapped her on the bottom. "Even a starving man wouldn't swap with Tom," he consoled her.

3

✳✳✳✳ They spent a quiet evening in the study. Katie read, Jeremy put some Mozart on the hi-fi. Her musical preferences did not run to his—the classics, including the three B's, Mozart, Wagner, Sibelius, but also Dixieland. But she could experience the music as a pleasant noise. It was too cool to sit outside and besides Olive barreled in, this time with a wedge of devil's food cake. The boys were driving her up the wall, she said, and Frank wouldn't be home until Friday night. Jeremy switched off the hi-fi, but Olive said, pushing her mop of impossibly scarlet hair from her high forehead, "Don't stop for me, Jeremy. Doug and Jim are in a fit of nostalgia—playing all the old Beatles records. And Lancelot's howling his fool head off."

She didn't stay long. She expected a call from Frank. After she left Jeremy went into the kitchen for a glass of milk. The devil's food cake was pretty good, he reported.

They went to bed and it was after midnight when the telephone rang. Jeremy rolled over, muttered crossly,

"We're closed," while Katie, alert as a bird dog, picked up the extension with one hand, touched the bedside lamp button with the other.

"Yes?"

A small mournful voice—one could only describe it as tear-stained—greeted her. "Mrs. Palmer? . . . This is Myra Emerich, I'm *so* sorry to call you at this *ghastly* hour. But Henry and I have been arguing ever since he came home for dinner." Her voice trailed off and Katie thought forlornly: Well, she lost. Me, too.

"Yes, Mrs. Emerich?"

"No use," said her no longer prospective client. "He's *adamant*. Put his foot down with a crash. He says he simply won't live in the backwoods, and that it would cost *thousands* to put the house and grounds into even fair shape."

Katie silently feared that he was right, and Mrs. Emerich went on, "I'm heartbroken, and so *apologetic* for taking up so much of your time, but I was almost *sure* he'd see it my way." Her voice brightened as she added, "He's promised to take me to Europe next month, for six weeks. And we do have friends who have bought houses over there, Spain, France—condominiums, too—marvelous for vacations and retirement and *much* less expensive living of course. I've friends in England, but Henry hates the climate. So we'll just rent a car and cruise around and—there's Portugal too and Majorca—and *look*, Henry's going to retire next year, he says. But I'm not so sure about that."

She went on talking and eventually, in reply to more apologies and "You've been so wonderful," Katie said, "It was my pleasure, Mrs. Emerich. I'm just sorry we're not to be neighbors—well—almost neighbors."

"I'll send postals," caroled Mrs. Emerich. "You're *such* a dear!"

"For God's sake!" exclaimed Jeremy, now awake but with his face in his pillow.

Katie, who knew she wouldn't sleep for the rest of the night, reached for the cigarettes which weren't there. She had given them up months ago.

She beat her pillow into a better support and said, "There goes the Grantson sale."

Jeremy rolled over again. "There'll be other suckers," he told her.

"Every agent I know has tried to sell it—it's a multiple listing, of course—but I came so close."

"You win a few and you lose a few."

"I can do without clichés," his wife informed him.

"Very well. Turn out the light and lie down. It's now Thursday. You have work to do; so have I, and we're going out to dinner."

When the light went out, he said gently, "I'm sorry, darling. You give so much to the agency and your clients. And I know you're sick with disappointment."

He put his arm around her. "Well," he added, smiling in the dark, "Now that we're both awake. . . ?"

In the morning after breakfast, Jeremy brought the car around, Lancelot barking busily behind it. "Drat that dog," he said mildly, "not that I don't like him, clumsy, friendly and, like me, always hungry."

"You had three eggs! Think of your cholesterol!"

"I'd rather not." He kissed her, opened the door and suggested, "Go to work."

"Drop you off?"

"Consider my physical fitness. . . . I thought you just did. I'll walk off the eggs."

"And the bacon?"

"Of course. . . . Have a good day. What time are we due at Jessica's?"

"Seven. Please get home in time to change."

"Why? Tweeds are beautiful."

Katie drove to the office, parked as usual and walked down the hill. It was a sparkling day; by noon it would be warm. She thought ruefully that the Andrews' pool would look inviting to any prospective buyer even in October.

She went in, greeted Flo, was told Mrs. Warner hadn't left yet and went in.

"You look tired," Emily said. "Up all night?"

"Some of it. Mrs. Emerich telephoned after twelve. Seems that her husband can't be convinced of the potential beauty of the Grantson property. So they're off to Europe next month to look over castles in Spain and elsewhere."

"There's a growing market for them, as you know. We've sold a few sight unseen." She sighed, "I'm sorry, Katie; you worked very hard."

"Everyone's worked hard."

Emily said, "In this business you don't give up. You're due at the Crowley closing, aren't you?"

"Yes . . . and Mrs. Crowley will have a list of questions, I suppose, most of which I can answer. And I'll take her to lunch——"

"Won't her daughters be with her?"

"Yes. They made the list. I'll take them, too," said Katie resigned.

Emily pondered. "The Pink Lantern," she decided. "It's just about right. Female food, fair service and drinks if anyone wants them."

Katie nodded and rose. She said, "I'm still stunned. Grantson seemed practically in the bag."

"If there's a spouse in the picture, male or female, it's always close." Emily looked at the clock. She said, "The Swans said they'd be here before eleven."

In honor of the Swans, her tailored dress was garnet red

and she wore an antique gold and garnet pin on her left shoulder.

"Good luck," said Katie, at the door.

"You don't mean it," Emily told her. "You'd like that place to stay untenanted until it falls down. It won't . . . fall, I mean, as most of it's been standing for about two hundred years. But thanks just the same. . . . Are you seeing the Redmond property this afternoon?"

"Yes." This was for inspection only, it had just come on the market, a three-year-old custom-built house, whose owner, like so many others, had been transferred.

"I've never seen it," said Emily. "Must take the time someday."

Katie went back to get her car and meet Mrs. Crowley and her anxious, devoted, somewhat overwhelming daughters at the lawyer's.

She had not mentioned Ross Cameron to Emily; she wouldn't unless the Swans weren't interested in the Andrews house.

In the afternoon, after an exhausting lunch, she saw Mrs. Crowley and her children off. Both young women were married, each had children and Mrs. Crowley was an enthusiastic charmer perfectly able to cope with a small house near the village, and with any help she needed. She wouldn't be resident in Little Oxford six weeks before she knew everyone by sight and everyone would know and love her. But to hear her girls talk you'd think her utterly helpless. What will Mother do when it snows, thunders, rains or if there were a fire, a power failure or someone broke in? And was Katie sure she'd given her the names and locations of the best shops, the names and numbers of the best doctors? Where was the hospital? Were there ambulances? Would Katie see to it that the telephone was connected as soon as possible?

From the restaurant parking space she watched Mrs. Crowley, all smiles, and her daughters, all melancholy, drive off. Mrs. Crowley was at the wheel.

Then Katie walked to the florist and selected two bright plants for clients who would be moving into their houses next week, and the florist said he'd be certain to have them there Wednesday afternoon.

She stopped at the office and Flo reported, "She's back, looking grim."

Katie's heart rose as she knocked and went in.

Emily said, "They didn't like it."

"I'm sorry."

"No, you're not. You look as if you were licking cream off your whiskers."

Katie said, "It's just that Jeremy has an old friend . . . we're seeing him tomorrow night." She couldn't resist adding, "He's taking us to the Saltmarsh for dinner. And he's looking for a house. I've told Jeremy that, as his friend's a bachelor, the Andrews house should be suitable. I'll tell him about it, and if he's interested, I could show it Saturday?"

She made that an inquiry, but she knew that Emily was to be in the city over the weekend.

"It's all yours, Katie. You can reach me in New York, or leave a message. Flo has the hotel and room number, and she can give you the keys." She smiled suddenly. "If you can't have the place yourself, the next best thing is to sell it to a friend, providing he can afford it."

"Jeremy says he can . . . but this is wishful thinking. All Jeremy said was that he'd had a phone call and his pal wanted a house in the area—and he's a bachelor—that is, he's divorced."

"So is Warren Andrews. . . . I'll call him when I get back. He was delighted when I told him about the Swans coming out to see the house." She sighed. "It will be easier to tell him that they disliked it if there's someone else interested. He's determined to sell, but at his own price. Rumor has it that he wants to remarry—this time a fantastically rich older woman who doesn't want any part of her native country. She's lived abroad for years. . . . Who is Jeremy's friend? An old customer?"

"His name's Ross Cameron. He and Jeremy were in the service together."

"Does he have children? That's no place for kids."

"One child," Jeremy said. "She lives with her mother."

"Personally," Emily said, "I don't like the house, attractive as it is. There's something about it—perhaps it was Warren —yes, definitely, Warren. You never knew him, did you?"

"No, he'd left here shortly before I came and the house was rented·until last year."

"For an incredible amount of money. Ask Amy Irvington about him someday. She was his secretary for a while before she worked at the hospital and married Ben. Do be at your most enchanting wide-eyed best when you see him—when is it—tomorrow night?"

"Yes." Katie smiled. Jeremy and his "beady little eyes," Emily and her "wide-eyed best." "I'll try," she promised.

"I'm sure of that. . . . Do you like escargots?"

"No—they're like rubber, but the sauce is great."

"Mussels?"

"Oh, yes."

"Then order the mussels vinaigrette and, if you like duck, the Saltmarsh chef cooks it to perfection. I always order it when I dine there. That's tough on the budget, as I'm usually the hostess. Before you go—I forgot to ask about Mrs. Crowley."

"She," said Katie, "is a doll. She'll be an asset to Little Oxford. The daughters are shattered that Mama is moving.

I suspect because she can no longer baby-sit. But I bet they'll be out weekends and call me up every hour on the hour. Their list of questions even includes: "Are you sure there aren't snakes in the backyard?" They've tried hard to convince Mrs. C she'll be lonely and in continual peril, but the lady has a mind of her own. She'll make a lot of friends; she has interests, drives her own car, and is dying to garden again—seems she lived in the country until her husband died. She's a churchgoer, too—and like everyone else she'll fall in love with Gordon Banks. She embroiders, loves to cook, plays canasta and golf!"

"Good. Run along home, Katie. . . . I'll keep my fingers crossed."

Katie went home. The towheaded twins were tossing a basketball into the basket outside of their part of the garage. Lancelot was racing around barking, as usual; the twins were quarreling, and Olive, on her back porch was howling at them, over Lancelot's yelps and a transistor, on a small outdoor table, tuned to fullest capacity.

As Katie came up her back steps, Olive said, "I simply can't do anything with them. Frank can, but he's home so seldom. . . . Boys, stop it this minute!"

They were now scuffling. One—Doug, probably, but Katie had trouble telling them apart—fell down, leaped up and seized his brother's long hair. They paid no attention to their mother.

Olive sat down on her steps and asked, "Why did I ever marry? . . . Come in for coffee, Katie?"

"I'd like to, but we're going out to dinner."

"Any place special?"

"The Bankses."

"Oh," said Olive, who belonged to another church. "He's so good-looking."

"He certainly is."

"What are you going to wear?"

"I've no idea. It's just dinner, and very informal—I don't know if anyone else will be there."

"I like that pageboy hairdo," Olive said.

"It's a revival," Katie reminded her, "sooner or later everything returns."

"Except virginity," Olive remarked glumly. "You doing anything special over the weekend?"

"Tomorrow night a friend of Jeremy's is taking us to the Saltmarsh place, Chez whatever it's called. I've never been there."

"Me either," Olive said. "I've tried to persuade Frank to take me out on our last three anniversaries, but he hates French cooking and says it's stupid to blow a whole week's commission just to eat dinner. Everytime I suggest something extravagant he reminds me that we have two kids to put through college—different colleges, seeing that they're twins —and providing they make it through high school and are accepted anywhere, and stay in." She paused. "Thank heaven for the pill," she remarked, "or I might have had—or still could have—another pair of borderline juvenile delinquents."

"They're not," Katie argued. "They're just healthy, lively, normal boys."

"That's what Frank says."

Katie walked up her steps and Olive said, "Be sure to tell me all about tomorrow night." She rose and advanced, with menace, upon her offspring, her wild hair cascading to her shoulders. "Wait till your father comes home . . ." she began.

Smiling, Katie went into her half house.

4

✳✳✳✳ When Jeremy came home, Katie was dressed and watching the clock. "You're late," she said.

"Not very. . . . Take a tranquilizer. Listen to music. Read a good book. I'll shower and change in no time flat."

So Katie sat in the living room, admiring, as she did every day, Jeremy's parents' beautiful low-keyed taste in furniture and thinking: If we're going to stay here for years, we must have new curtains. Such a pity that those from the brownstone couldn't be made to fit. She picked up a magazine and leafed through it, wondering what she'd wear tomorrow night.

Jeremy came downstairs, asking, "Where's your coat?" He gave her a rib-crushing hug and remarked complacently, "I'm so glad I married a woman who doesn't scream, 'Be careful of my lipstick, and please don't disturb my hair.'"

"Repairs," Katie commented, "are easy. Have you known many such foolish women?"

"Quite a few. But if we start talking about my past, we'll never get to the Bankses. Incidentally, don't ever listen to Ross if he gets on the subject of our mutual girl chasing . . . actually, I chased, and he *was* chased without the t."

He helped her with her coat; she picked up her handbag and they went out to the car. On the way he told her, "The Irvingtons will be there tonight."

"How did you discover that?"

"Doctor Bing Irvington came tearing into the shop today looking for a book his wife wants. . . . we had it. . . . They'll both be there, and the young Irvingtons also."

Ben Irvington was the Palmers' doctor. He had taken over a good deal of his father's practice, and all the newer patients. Katie was fond of him and of his wife whom she had come to knew well, when, moving from the Irvington guesthouse, they had looked for, and found, a good little rental. Now they owned a couple of acres, bought with part of the legacy Ben's maternal grandmother had left him, and hoped some-day to build.

"Amy," said Jeremy, "will probably bring the baby in a basket. Doesn't trust baby-sitters."

"Jessica will love that. She always deplores the fact that, although two of her three children are married, there are no little ones."

He asked curiously, "You don't really like Jessica, do you?"

Of course, I like her," Katie answered indignantly. "She's kind and warm and so lovely to look at, but . . ."

"But what?"

"She scares me. When she looks at me with those big violet eyes, I feel that she sees right through me."

"Maybe she does," said Jeremy, "but, what she sees, I'm sure she likes." He added, "Some years ago—before I knew you—she was very ill. Dr. Irvington—Bing that is—pulled her through. Gordon was beside himself. She still looks frail, but she's fine actually."

"It must be tough being married to a clergyman," Katie remarked thoughtfully.

"I used to think it was—for her. I don't now. He's changed a good deal since her illness. . . . I didn't see much of them in those days, but I could sense the change. And he's a great man in the pulpit. I wish you'd come to church with me more often."

"I do when I can—but Sundays are difficult for me— Saturdays and Sundays, clients——"

"I know, and so do the Bankses."

The parsonage in which the Gordon Bankses lived was big, as were the church and the parish hall where they had meetings and social activities and where Gordon had his office.

Big church, big house, big parish—a very substantial one— and Gordon Banks was a big man. He had a fine speaking voice and an arresting face beneath thick white hair. He was at the door when they drove up and parked in the ample space beside Doctor Irvington's car.

"Hi," said Jeremy. "If we're late, it's my fault."

"You're not late and Jessica is busy having quiet raptures over Amy's redheaded baby."

He took Katie's coat and they all went into the big living room, where Doctor Irvington, known to friends and patients as Bing, greeted them, and his wife Letty kissed Katie's cheek and said, "I haven't seen you in ages."

Katie looked at them with affection, the tall man with silver-copper hair, the small woman with gilt and silver curls. She asked, "Is Ben here?"

"No, he'll be late. Amy's with Jessica. How long since you have seen Benjy the third?"

"Oh, about three weeks."

"He's grown a foot," said Benjy's grandmother, leading the way into a small sitting room where Benjy was graciously dispensing smiles, chuckles, and occasional sharp sounds of discontent from a basket. He was eight months old.

Amy Irvington—a delightful young woman, and a very happy one—left her son's side and embraced Katie. She asked, "Why don't you stop in now and then? I've managed to buy some furniture—antique, early American. Ben's apoplectic. He keeps reminding me that since I stopped working, he has to work ten times as hard. Now, come look at our tax deduction."

Obediently Katie looked; she was terrified of babies, and when Jessica said, "You can pick him up; he won't break," Katie shook her head. "I'd drop him," she admitted. But Jeremy reached into the basket and hauled young Benjy out. Accustomed to his father and grandfather and, for that matter, his great-grandfather, Benjy obliged by squealing and then falling asleep against Jeremy's shoulder.

Katie experienced a guilty moment. She thought: Jeremy does love kids. "But not yet," she told herself. "There's plenty of time."

During dinner—while Benjy, in his basket, slept, wept or laughed—his father appeared, saying, "Hi everyone, I'm starved—also beat." He ran his hands through his red hair. "Why didn't you tell me it's a dog's life, Pop?"

"I did, and for some years now you've been telling me. What, or who, beat you?"

"Old Mrs. Trowbridge. She's never really accepted me," said Ben sadly.

"I'll go see her tomorrow, socially," his father assured him.

Food was furnished and Ben said, "Don't mind me, folks. Go ahead with your social chatter and fattening dessert. . . . How's my son and heir?"

"Asleep," his wife reported, "for the moment."

When they'd returned to the living room, Gordon said, "Ran into your grandfather yesterday, Ben, walking down the road. I stopped to talk with him. He looks better than he did. I hope he's going to be content here."

"Well, he didn't much like living abroad," Ben said. "I think he was always homesick for Little Oxford. But Gram wouldn't come home except on visits. Her death, of course, was almost a mortal blow to him."

Letty's eyes filled. She said, "I'm so grateful that my mother went quickly. . . . No one who ever knew her could have tolerated the thought of long suffering and invalidism —least of all, father, but I do think he's as happy here as he could be anywhere now. . . . He didn't like France much."

Ben looked at his mother. "Gramp always expected to die first," he said. "He couldn't imagine being alone or that any-one as vital as Gram could leave this earth. I'm glad he sold the house—even if he dispossessed Amy and me. . . . It's great to have him with us, here, at home."

"You needed a bigger house, anyway," Letty reminded him.

Amy and the baby, who had come in the older Irving-tons' car, left with Ben, and presently Jeremy said, "Hate to leave, but tomorrow's a busy day." And Bing said, smil-ing, "We'll have to stagger home alone, Letty. So far, no impatient patient for Ben or me. I suspect, once we get home, answering service will make up for that. So let's stay awhile.

I'm very comfortable where I am. Perhaps the service has forgotten Gordon's number."

"No chance," said Letty.

On the way back to Baker Street Jeremy remarked, "What a fine satisfactory evening. We're really fortunate to live here and to have such good friends."

Katie made an assenting murmur.

"You're curiously quiet, Katie," her husband told her. "Anything wrong?"

"I was just thinking."

"Plotting your raid on Cam's bank account!"

"Cam?"

"Ross then, but everyone calls him Cam."

"Oh! . . . No, I was thinking about you."

"A step in the right direction. What about me?"

"Just that you were so taken with Amy's baby . . . and have been every time you see him."

"I like babies—also kittens, puppies, cubs."

"Be serious. You feel that I'm depriving you, don't you?"

He said carefully, "It was understood before we married that you wouldn't contemplate having children for some time. I agreed to that."

"But you aren't happy about it."

"Let's just say, I'm happy with you."

"But not completely."

He said, exasperated, "Who's completely happy? Oh, I'm sure you could name dozens who are happy, including both sets of Irvingtons—but never completely. Everyone, married or single, has hang-ups, makes compromises, adjusts. In our case I've had to compromise. Now you've had two years of it—your way."

"We didn't set a date!"

"I know. But while we're young—"

"I'll still be young in two more years, even in four!"

He said, as if he hadn't heard her, "You don't have to work. I make a profit, and there's a good anchor to windward. I thought, once you decided to quit, and start a family, we'd buy or build. That's one reason I didn't want the Andrews house. It isn't a place for children, quite aside from the fact that I don't like it."

"I don't want to quit. I like working, and I'd hate being solely dependent on you."

"The liberated woman who has her own bank account, so she can walk out tomorrow. How come you permit me to pay rent, utilities, food and taxes?"

She said, angered, "I offered to pay my share whenever I could."

"So you did. But that isn't my idea of marriage."

"Of course not——"

"So, I'm a male chauvinist?"

"Bordering on that," Katie said furiously.

"Okay. And you alone have the right to decide when we have children?"

"I certainly do. I'd be the one walking around, sick, looking like a balloon, risking my life, going through nine months of being scared, and, I'm told, with good reason."

He said after a moment, "All right, Katie, but I hoped such a decision, either way, would be mutual."

She was silent as they turned into their driveway. Jeremy put the car away, tripped over a bike and swore savagely as he came into the house. This was the first time since before their marriage that the subject of children had been discussed. Blame it on Benjy.

Jeremy turned off the rear porch light, went through to the front door and turned off that light. Katie had gone upstairs, leaving the hall lights on for him. He switched them off and went on up. His wife was sitting at her dressing table, brushing her hair, a morning and night performance which had not ceased to enchant him. Her face was flushed, and her small jaw set, but she had not been crying; she rarely cried.

He said, "I almost fell over the boys' bikes."

"So what's new?" inquired Katie. "You do it almost every time you put the car away. You could speak to the twins, you know, or their parents."

"I've tried."

He walked about undressing, emptying his pockets of change, sitting down on the bed to take off his shoes.

"Bad for the mattress," said Katie coldly, watching him in the mirror. She thought: If only he'd fight, really fight, yell at me, throw things, but no, he's always so damned reasonable.

Jeremy did not move to a chair. He took off his shoes, carefully hung up his clothes and, in slippers and what Katie had once called his "essential lingerie," disappeared into the bathroom. She thought, brushing furiously: Also he's too neat. Her own belongings were strewn, haphazard round the big room. She'd pick them up tomorrow. Or if he did it, as he often did, tonight she'd murder him.

Reasonable, tidy, hard-working, intelligent, fun to be with and so attractive. Revolting, she thought, and almost laughed at her own inconsistency.

Jeremy returned in his pajamas, walked over and touched her bare shoulder. He said. "Katie, one of the unforgettable things my father told me was, 'After you're married'—I was about seventeen at the time—'never go to bed mad.' "

Katie said stonily, "I'm not mad."

"You're mad, all right." He lifted her from the dressing-table bench and held her. "No, you don't," said Katie, struggling.

"Then," said Jeremy, "we'll sit up, for the rest of the night."

"But I'm tired," Katie wailed.

"Of course. And tomorrow you have houses to sell, and clients to run errands for and you must look your best for Cam and the Chez Expensive or whatever it is at Saltmarsh." He carried her over to the bed and dumped her on it.

"You turned down the bed," she said accusingly.

"Yes, in the usual sense."

"And put out my nightgown?"

"Of course. Gives a nice homey touch. Anyway, don't I generally?"

"Yes. You're a perfectly infuriating man."

"Agreed," said Jeremy amiably. He switched off lights except the nightstand lamp on his side of the bed.

"Forget this evening," he suggested, "that is to say the latter part of it. Kiss me and I'll let you go to sleep right now if you wish."

After a moment she said, "I don't wish."

5

✳✳✳✳ Friday was the essence of October . . . the sky, a pure blue; white clouds drifting with a small wind, altering shapes; the foliage burning steadily brighter. Presently there would be the long weekend, and the tours through New England, with people looking from bus windows, exclaiming over this passage through fire before the gray days, the white days, and the resurrection of spring.

The sun was warm, even early in the morning, and Jeremy brought coffee, rolls, crisp bacon and a jar of honey to the sun deck. Katie was up and wrapped in a warm long robe as he had said firmly, when he woke her, "Breakfast in the open air. There won't be many more Saturdays."

A red leaf, a yellow and one still stubbornly green, had drifted over the railing and were on the floor. "A good day for selling a couple of houses and a flock of books," said Jeremy. "Pretty soon everyone will want to curl up in a new house and watch the snow, or read a new book. . . . You all right, Katie?"

She said, "Great," and stirred her coffee, looking at him with wide, serious eyes. With her hair in a topknot and a morning-scrubbed face, she looked very young and he smiled at her, thinking of last night, of the two years they'd spent together, of the years ahead. She knew that expression and it stirred her to answering tenderness, and also to exasperation.

She said, "You're thinking about last night."

"Right."

"No it wasn't," said Katie. "And that's as much my fault as yours."

He raised an eyebrow. "What's that supposed to mean?" he asked and a small sense of anxiety nudged at him sharply.

"Not what you're thinking," she began hastily. "I mean, it solved nothing; it's too easy."

"Was there anything to solve?"

"Of course."

"Eat something, Katie."

"I'm not hungry." She pushed the rolls and bacon toward him. "You eat while it's still hot."

He poured himself more coffee. "Just what's bugging you, Katie?" he asked.

"I don't know. . . . Yes, I do, a little. I love you," she said quietly. "I love having breakfast with you, sleeping with you, laughing with you . . . but I don't think I like being married."   .

"Why not?"

He regarded her thoughtfully. They'd been married two years; they'd known each other for a while before that. He didn't, of course, really know her. That takes ten, twenty, forty years. He looked forward to it.

Katie shrugged. She said, "Well, take last evening for instance."

He said, commendably patient. "Why? There's no way—at least in this era—that I can force you into having a child. Nor would I want to if I could."

"Forget it," Katie said. She rose abruptly, went over to him and kissed the top of his head. "I have to get dressed, Jeremy. I've a dozen things to do in the office and out."

She went back into the bedroom, showered, dressed, made the bed. Jeremy had picked up her belongings, she noted with irritation.

She heard him washing up downstairs and thought: Why can't he just stack the dishes for once?

When they were in the car, she asked, "What time is Mr. Cameron picking us up?"

"He isn't. We're calling for him at the Inn at seven and driving him to the superb clip joint. He'll reserve a table. Cam reserves everything—a diner booth, a bar stool or a blonde down the corridor."

"Be serious. I thought you said he was driving up?"

"He is—in a rental car. One of his is garaged somewhere on the Island at his brother's; the other's currently being overhauled in Manhattan."

"I can't wait to meet him."

"Contain yourself, darling. . . . See you later."

Katie spent a busy day. She saw one possible client, ran errands for others, did some paper work, and when she came home, called her mother upstate, "Are you all right?" her mother asked.

"Fine. Just busy. That's why I haven't written."

Talking with her, Katie could visualize her mother, short, pleasantly round, full of bounce and projects, alone in the too big house, sitting at the telephone in the kitchen.

"How's Jeremy?"

"He's charming, absent-minded and in excellent health, as usual."

"I wish you'd come up for a weekend."

"You know weekends are my busiest time until winter . . . and Jeremy works Saturdays. Why don't you come down here before it starts snowing?"

"I'm busy too," Susan Norton said. "Church, garden club, volunteer work. Besides, what would I do?"

"You've friends here," said Katie, "and you had fun last time. Jeremy can always use an unpaid worker in the shop. I'd drive you around the countryside. You could cook—Jeremy thinks you're a fabulous cook—and also, you sew, I have closets full of stuff needing repair. Drive down and bring your machine; just let me know ahead. We'd love having you."

"I'll consider it. . . . I don't know how Jeremy stands you, Katie."

Katie laughed. She said, "Sometimes I can't stand him."

"Naturally. Marriage," Mrs. Norton said, "is constitutional . . . the pursuit of happiness, and also, equal opportunity."

"What do you mean, 'equal opportunity'?"

"Think it over. This is costing money. I'll write. Goodbye, dear. Much love to you both."

Katie hung up, smiling. She was very fond of her mother, but, she often thought: How did Father endure her? Susan Norton was, and had always been, like an uncertain wind in the house, blowing hot, blowing cold. She did a dozen things, all well. When neighbors were in difficulties, they came to Susan Norton. She dispensed advice without sentimentality. Now and then she blew the roof off. But Katie's father had regarded his wife as a paragon of all the virtues; he'd been a quiet, slow-moving, and in some ways, rather helpless man.

Jeremy came home earlier than usual and found Katie fresh out of the tub, in her warm robe, regarding the contents of her clothes closet. He said, "Hi. Not dressed yet?"

"Plenty of time. And I don't know what to wear."

Jeremy cast himself into a chair and said, as she removed a long frock from its hanger and held it up against her, "Not that. We aren't going to Buckingham Palace or the Country Club Christmas dance."

They didn't belong to the Country Club. Jeremy had refused to put his name on the waiting list. "Like sweating it out until your draft number comes up," he'd remarked, when she'd suggested it. "Besides, who needs it?"

Katie thought now, as she often did: We do. Oh, they went there occasionally as guests of friends, with Jeremy muttering, "Dandy." Now, he advised, "Short. Becoming. Casual, but not too casual." He pointed a long finger. "There. . . . That pale green job with the full skirt."

Katie rehung the long dress, removed the green one from its hanger. "How come you know so much?" she inquired.

"My customers. They gather in small vocal knots and yak. I have good hearing."

Katie put the dress on the bed, and sat down beside it. "I called mother a little while ago," she told him.

"How is she? Any signs of remarriage?"

"None, unfortunately."

"Why unfortunately? You don't like marriage," he reminded her.

"But she was so *used* to it," said Katie. "Besides she shouldn't be alone in that house. I wish she'd sell it."

"It means a lot to her, Katie, and she isn't alone with one dog, three cats and neighbors."

"Just the same I worry. . . . Suppose something happens;

she might fall downstairs. Oh, my," she added, horrified, "I'm talking like the Crowley girls."

"Who?"

"I told you about them. Their mother's moved here and they drove me up the wall dreaming up things which might happen to her, living here in the boondocks alone. . . . Mother sent you her love."

"Good. When is she coming down?"

"I don't know. I asked her. She says she's busy, but she'll consider it."

"I could do with a Susan Norton boiled dinner," Jeremy said sadly.

Katie drew up her knees, wrapped her arms around them and reported, "Mother said she doesn't know how you stand me."

"And of course you told her you often couldn't stand me?"

"Well . . . yes. But she reminded me that marriage is equal opportunity."

"Of course it is."

"Do I irritate you?"

"Sometimes."

"What do I do?"

"File your nails when I'm trying to read. Then there's your passion for disk jockeys. It's a modest list of 'I wish she wouldn't . . .' How about yours? . . . No don't tell me; I'll tell you. I am revoltingly neat. I'm a better cook and housekeeper. I get steamed up about books that you wouldn't open, much less understand, if you did. I have fits of abstraction. I forget things important to you. I dislike country clubs and you hate the way in which I eat a boiled egg!"

Katie regarded him with astonishment. "How did you know—about the egg. I mean?"

"It's not your way," he reminded her. "I stand mine up in the small end of my cherished ironstone eggcup, tap it with a knife, then firmly slice off the end and eat the rest from the shell with a very small spoon. I can't help it. My mother had an English Nanny. Admit that you hate it, Katie."

"I don't, exactly. It's only that I always know just what you're going to do."

He said cheerfuly, "Always? Then you're luckier than most wives. But the problem isn't insurmountable. I can break my egg into a regular cup, after this, just as you do. Messy, but I'll get used to it."

"Jeremy, I never said anything about it except on our wedding trip when I just asked you how come? You explained then, as you did now, so how did you know——"

"Oh, you have methods of conveying slight disturbances. Your eyelashes flutter, or you give an almost invisible start or shudder, and your brows are faintly creased."

Now she was laughing. She said, "I'll try to be less transparent." She hopped off the bed. "It's time to dress."

"Hold on." He rose, took hold of her. "There's a sort of formula," he stated, "an antidote to most of the small exasperations which upset man and wife. Just tell yourself, 'But I love him in spite of the manner in which he consumes a breakfast egg.' And I'll tell myself: 'Even though the sound of a file rasping against fingernails afflicts my nerves, I love her.' I don't say that large irritations will respond to this prescription, or that real problems will be solved, but there's one thing I can predict——"

"Are you in a trance?" she asked solicitously.

"No. Jessica would say, 'I have an impression.' So I have an impression. After we've been married fifty years or so and one of us dies. . . ."

46

"Don't say that!"

"Okay. When one of us ascends to his or her ancestors—what the other one will remember with unbearable grief will be the unimportant things, as well as the important; the irritations as well as the delight . . . the egg, the rasping file." He kissed her and released her. "Go make yourself beautiful for Cam," he suggested, "and don't spare the horses. You want to please your husband's friend and also sell him a house, don't you?"

He loped away to find slacks, a rather wild shirt which Katie had given him, jacket and tie, and Katie, brushing her hair at the dressing table, found that her eyes were bright wells of tears.

Life with Jeremy was often difficult—and could get worse—but life without Jeremy would be unthinkable.

6

✳✳✳✳ "How do I look?"

"Perfectly awful."

"Thanks. You're sweet."

"I used the adjective correctly. You fill me with awe, Sabrina fair."

"Didn't she come to a bad end?" Katie inquired.

"No. Lord knows what you studied in college, but you must have encountered Milton in high school."

Katie said dreamily, "There was a boy named Milton in my class—he was gorgeous. Tell me more about Sabrina."

"She had," Jeremy told her, " 'amber drooping hair'. . . . For heaven's sake, it's past time to go."

Katie picked up the little mink cape which had been his present to her on her recent birthday. On the first birthday after their marriage he had turned in her rather beat-up car and bought her a new one, "in the interest of your profession," he had told her.

There was ample room in the front seat for three. Jeremy

drove through the village to the Inn, which was set well back from a wide semi-country road, and parked. "Sit there," he said. "I'll fetch Cam."

When a few minutes later he returned to the car with his friend, Katie saw in the ineffectual light a man not nearly as tall as Jeremy, but one who stood so erect that he seemed almost as tall; Jeremy stooped, a little. She caught a glimpse of a wide, warm smile; and white teeth in a tanned face. The introductions were brief—"Katie, Cam . . . Cam, Katie. . . . Climb in, Cam; we'll put Katie in the middle."

On the way to Saltmarsh, the men talked and Katie listened. Finally she asked, "How long since you've seen each other?"

"Oh, more than two years, when I was in town and we had lunch. He's a difficult character to pin down; he's always somewhere else."

Cam had a good resonant voice. He said, "Don't give Katie the impression that I scurry off on yachts with the beautiful people. But I am away a good deal. We have offices in Chicago, San Francisco, and Atlanta, and since I'm vice president in charge of paper clips and water coolers, my father sends me hither and yon to see that everything's in order. I rather like it, Jeremy. After I was settled at the Inn—nice place, I remember it from some years ago—I walked to the village and peered in windows. The place has grown since my friends, the Howards, lived here. Incidentally, I spent a few moments in front of your windows. Lovely display."

"Books? But you don't read anything but the *Wall Street Journal*."

"I read a great deal," Cam said reproachfully. "*Playboy*, magazines about cars, and an occasional shocker—I'm always trying to improve myself. Seriously, I didn't notice the books because there was a young woman in the window, rearranging things. She, however, needs no rearrangement."

"Betty Nelson," said Jeremy. "She's the newest and youngest of the current staff."

"Five-five," remarked Cam, "or thereabouts; thirty-six—twenty-three—thirty-six approximately. Red hair."

"I'm not privy to her vital statistics," Jeremy told him. "I keep forgetting to borrow Katie's tape measure."

Katie was laughing. She asked, "Did you establish her weight, too, Cam?"

"About one hundred and twelve, wouldn't you say?"

"I haven't seen her yet."

"Just as well. Who is she?"

"A young widow," Jeremy told him.

"Young widows are poison," Cam remarked.

"Beth's not. She's a good hard-working sweet-tempered gal," Jeremy told him. "She married, went with her husband to a camp in the Southwest where he was killed on a training flight. So she came back here to live with her parents."

"I'll avoid your shop," Cam said. "As you said, I have no taste for the literary. And having been freed from the universal trap, I recoil from young widows, mothers with eligible daughters, and anxious divorcees."

"That must curtail your social life," Katie observed thoughtfully. "Unless you enjoy the company of the elderly."

Cam said carelessly, "On the contrary, I enjoy walking around the traps. Amazing how skillful one becomes in the battle for self-preservation."

"Katie," said Jeremy, "confines her reading to *Real Estate Principles and Practices* and *Questions and Answers on Real Estate*. Fascinating. In her lighter moments she devours mysteries."

Cam asked, "Did you ever sell a haunted house, Katie?"

"Once. At least the buyer thought it haunted, which was one reason why she bought it; she likes ghosts."

"I think the word is spirits," Jeremy said, "such as brandy, vodka, bourbon."

When they reached Chez Nous, which was a long low structure "commanding a view of the endangered Saltmarsh and polluted water," as Jeremy remarked cheerfully, they were escorted to a window table and Katie had her first clear look at their host. He had a quantity of brown hair, worn a little long, and eyes which were hazel green. The brown skin came from sun or sunlamps. His prominent nose had once been broken, she decided, and he had unusually fine hands. She said, when the drinks had been ordered, "I don't understand it."

"What exactly?" Jeremy asked.

"Why you two are such good friends; you're very different."

Cam, regarding her thoughtfully, said, "You didn't tell me that she's beautiful, Jeremy."

"She isn't, really," Jeremy answered. "It's simply that she gives that impression. It comes from self-confidence and the constant attention of a devoted husband, making for security."

The drinks came and he raised his glass, "To reunion in Saltmarsh," he said. "As to us being different, Katie, that's the answer. I couldn't stomach a friend like myself."

Looking at the menu, Katie saw Mrs. Warner's mussels and duck but selected, in their stead, a lobster cocktail and filet mignon. Mrs. Warner could dictate to her in the office.

She was saddened when both Cam and Jeremy had ordered the mussels and the duck.

Cam said casually toward the end of an excellent dinner, "I understand you're going to sell me a house."

Katie smiled. "I'm going to try—that is if you wish. I think we have a listing which will interest you."

"It probably won't," Cam warned her. "I'm perfectly content with my apartment, but something came over me recently and I thought perhaps a little country place would be a healthy change. What about the house—is it on the water?"

"No. But it has a pool, and ample room for a bachelor—and his guests. It's old, but in good condition, and it has all the modern conveniences. It belongs to a writer who is now living abroad."

"Has it just come on the market?"

"No."

"So why hasn't it sold?"

She said candidly, "The asking price, for one thing; for another, it isn't suitable for people with children."

"What day's tomorrow? Oh—Saturday. Can you show it to me then?"

"I'd be delighted," Katie said and Cam, looking at Jeremy, remarked, "You understand I may not be as interested as I think I am or seem. This is just an excuse to have a little time alone with your wife."

"I comprehend perfectly," said Jeremy. "This place is Katie's dream house. She's been cajoling, imploring, even ordering me to buy it ever since we were married, even before, when she asked me to marry her."

"I did *not* ask you to marry me!"

"In a manner of non-speaking."

Cam laughed. He asked, "Well, why didn't you buy it?"

"For the excellent reasons she mentioned. They apply to me as well as to other Warner clients. The owner of course wants too much money and there isn't enough room for the patter of little feet—although the current generation must have been born with outsize pedal extremities, judging by the young who invade the bookshop. There's also another reason—I don't like the place. Great house to visit, but I'd hate to live there."

Katie looked balefully at her husband.

"As you and Cam appear to have great rapport," she said, "you are deliberately discouraging him."

"His tastes and mine aren't similar," Jeremy said cheerfully. "Besides I think that the elegant little joint would be fine for him."

Cam asked curiously, "What's this about the patter of little feet? As the father of one brilliant, beautiful, spoiled and sometimes obnoxious girl child, I'm interested."

Jeremy said, "Four kids would be about right, and eventually we'll buy or build, suitably."

"How about you, Katie?" Cam asked.

Katie shook her head, "Jeremy's a dreamer," she answered. "How old is your little girl?"

Cam sighed. "Nine. Unlike Jeremy, I married as soon as we came out of the service. I should have known better. I'm a couple of years older than your 'look before you leap' husband."

"What's her name?"

"Veronica Caldwell Ross, named for my former wife's rich grandmother. Unfortunately, Grandma spent it while she had it, all the time living up to the legend, hence surrounded by solicitous children. All Ronnie inherited was a singularly hideous silver tea set."

Later, as they deposited Cam on the Inn's colonial doorstep, he had suggested that Katie pick him up at ten the next morning. "I refuse to be biased by my old comrade in arms," he told her. "At one time, despite my seniority and superior sophistication, he had great influence over me. He was logical, sober—most of the time—and persuasive. He did a lot for me, did Jeremy, always for my own good. But nothing is more infuriating, after you've had time to think it over."

On the way to Baker Street, Jeremy asked, "What do you think of him?"

"Very attractive," Katie answered promptly, "and likable. If he buys here—and I hope he does—he'll create a considerable stir."

"Among the women you mean—old and young, of course. He always has. But, as he told us, he's become wary and adept, an artful dodger."

"Did you know his wife?"

"Sybil? Naturally. I was his best man. I even warned him against her, but that time he didn't listen. He had known her before he went into the service."

"What's she like?"

"As of now, I don't know; then, she was rather like his description of Veronica—all but the brilliant, that is—beautiful, spoiled, and sometimes obnoxious. Also, she didn't need her grandmother's vanished money."

"House or no house, it was a fun evening," Katie remarked.

"A most revolting expression," Jeremy told her. "Do I need to warn you?"

"About what?"

"Not about—against. Cam's a great guy. I'm fond of him. But from what he told me last time I saw him—and which I already knew—he leans toward safely married women, careful of course not to get himself into deep water. Most complacent husbands don't mind—especially the busy ones who haven't time nor inclination to attend the concert, the ballet, the parties. Cam's in great demand. But I'm sure that he would hare off, if the lady decided her husband didn't understand her."

54

Katie said, "You're smug!"

"Nope."

"And you don't understand me."

"Also negative. Still, take heart. Cam won't either. But there's a difference, I expect, when several decades have passed. Forty years with the same woman, for instance, is more conducive to understanding than forty women in the same amount of time."

"You're an idiot," she said, and put her hand over his on the wheel.

As they were going to bed, he stated, rather than asked, "You're pretty excited about tomorrow's possibilities."

"Naturally. But I'm not dancing around strewing flowers. This happens almost every day—the prospective client—and I'm learning to subdue my hopes. You didn't tell me that your Beth Nelson was so attractive."

"She's not mine. I did tell you when I hired her, but you were lying on the bed, with the radio on your flat little stomach, listening to one of your DJs."

"Just how attractive is she?"

"Cam told you. In my opinion, she's decorative, also useful. In her work, calm, collected, friendly, and an asset. . . . As you know, we have a number of male customers, and since she's been around, they drift in oftener. Perhaps those who patronize the lending library—which is as much Beth's responsibility as her older confreres—have learned to read faster, by page and paragraph. Anyway, while I'm not in a position to guide their reading, the best-seller lists, the reviews, word of mouth, and helpful help at the shop all do that. It seems to me that they are now devouring everything on the shelves like so many silverfish."

"I really must find time to stop in and get a good look at this paragon."

"Do," he invited courteously, "and when you get around

to it, we'll have her here for dinner, as we've had the others. I'll cook," he added hastily. "Now, for heaven's sake, come to bed. You've a house to sell tomorrow."

"God—and Cameron Ross—willing," Katie qualified piously.

7

✳✳✳✳ Katie had hoped for a sparkling day, a backdrop of impossibly blue skies, enriched with whipped-cream clouds, with bushes and trees flaming busily, against which setting Cam would view the house. But it was Saturday and like a great many country Saturdays had turned sullen, possibly to discourage tourists, weekend houseguests and irascible children. The wind was cold and the sky, gray, except when it relented for a moment of sunlight. Picking up Cam at the Inn, she apologized.

"Seems as if I toil around showing places to people, a good three-quarters of the time in rain, snow flurries, heat, or, like today, when anything can happen."

"Compose yourself," Cam advised. "When you sell under adverse, but natural, circumstances, that's a real triumph. Sunlight exposes cracks, peeling paint, dust and other defects."

"Mr. Andrews has a caretaker," Katie said. "He doesn't live in, but he's around a good deal of each day, checking on wiring, doors, windows, the pool—he hasn't emptied it yet—spider webs, dust, landscaping. If he's there when we arrive, his name is Mr. Jackson. He doesn't answer to 'Hi' or any loud cry."

"What in the world possessed you to go into real estate?"

"Necessity, after my father died and I left college. I had an uncle who was already in it and I dreamed of becoming a partner one day. His son—my cousin Dick whom I cordially dislike—was off making his fortune in California, Alaska, Ohio—you name it. He didn't make it in any state so he came home to learn, and eventually inherit the business, although he had vowed before he went into the service that if he returned alive he wouldn't set foot in the home town, that he hated houses, commercial properties, land, lawyers, the works."

"Where was all this?"

She told him, adding, "I had a friend in Little Oxford, so I came here."

"I bet you looked at a map and decided on a prosperous, growing, top-drawer town within commuting distance of the city."

"Of course," said Katie.

"How does Jeremy like your working?"

"Well, I was working when he met me at his cousins', the Gordon Bankses—do you know them?"

"No. . . . Do you know a Mrs. William Niles?"

Katie answered, astonished, "I know of her, of course. She's legendary in Little Oxford. I've even seen her on the street, and the Bankses know her very well. Wherever did you meet her?"

"Oh, a long time ago in Paris. She had a protégé with her —a girl she'd installed there in a little apartment. She had great faith in the child's future as a singer, and had enrolled her—if that's what one does—with one of the best teachers in Europe."

Katie said, "I heard about that. . . . Look, here we are."

As they arrived, the sun came out to shed fleeting sequins on the swimming pool and an elderly man in a checked wool shirt and blue jeans was working around the hedges.

"Looks pleasant," Cam remarked.

Mr. Jackson approached. He said, "Morning, Miz Palmer."

"This is Mr. Ross," she said. "We're here to see the house, Mr. Jackson."

Mr. Jackson's alert blue gaze fastened on Cam for a moment and seemed to sum up his failures, successes, income, morals and intentions. He said, "Pleased to meet you. . . . You got the key, Miz Palmer?"

"Yes," she said smiling. Cam smiled and Mr. Jackson's lips twitched almost as if he, too, would smile. He said, "Had to get leaves outta the pool. The man ain't been around this past week. He thought I'd drain it, but I was waiting till next week in case someone come by."

"I'm glad you did," Cam said, looking at the pool and the patio, and Jackson said hastily, "I put up the patio furniture. We'll have rain soon, or maybe even snow."

Katie produced the key and they went into the house. It was cool, but not too cool. She said, "Because of the furniture, Mr. Andrews keeps the place properly heated. If you're cold, I'll ask Jackson to adjust the thermostat. . . . It's electric heat, by the way."

"What happens when the power goes off?"

She'd heard that question from so many people in so many houses that she was waiting for it. In this case, she was able to say, "There's a generator in the cellar."

Going in, she warned him, "It isn't very big."

Square hall, living room, dining room and then, attached to the old house by a breezeway, the Andrews study. Cam inspected each room, and asked, "He's just storing his furniture here?"

"He wants to sell it with the house or, if the buyer doesn't want it, there's a good antique dealer in the village."

"This was his study?"

"Yes. A well-known architect designed it for him. You can see how, outside and in, it conforms perfectly with the old house. His books are gone"—she gestured to the empty shelves—"and his files. I understand that his agent arranged to have the books, files, and the paintings—there were two, a Klee, in the living room, and a Wyeth in here—shipped to the city for storage. Oh, and some prints, hunting mostly."

Cam walked around, looking and opening doors. Katie said, "That's a full bath. This unit would make a good guest room—there aren't many book shelves to come out, if a buyer didn't want them; the paneling beneath is quite lovely. There are other shelves in the living room, as you've seen, and in the bigger bedroom, upstairs."

"Well let's try upstairs," Cam suggested.

He smiled slightly, prowling about. He didn't overlook anything, Katie noticed. His expression was unreadable, to her annoyance. The master bedroom was furnished in old pieces, all severely masculine. Cam said, "I see the curtains up here have been washed and those downstairs cleaned. Thoughtful of him."

Katie said, "Mrs. Warner has seen to it that the house can be lived in as of tomorrow."

The attached bath was part dressing room with closets built in, shelves for sweaters and cupboards for shoes.

"Whoever remodeled this," Cam remarked, "did a very good job."

Entering the smaller of the bedrooms, he whistled. Twin beds, and very feminine decor. The bathroom was also half dressing room, and had mermaid wallpaper and gold-plated fixtures. "Well, well," said Cam. "I suppose he kept this for his aged mama or his spinster sisters?"

"If he had an aged mama or sisters," Katie agreed gravely.

"This is all?"

"Not quite." They went back into the wide hall. There were faded patches where the prints had hung—more book-shelves and two straight, beautiful chairs.

"What else?"

"There's an apartment over the garage. It was built for a couple. Mr. Andrews had just one man living in. It's attractive. It could even be rented if necessary."

"Let's go."

They went downstairs and outdoors. The sun looked at them briefly, disapproved and hid behind a cloud; the ruffled pool water ceased its brief sparkle.

Mr. Jackson was still in evidence. He looked across a hedge expectantly, and Katie asked, "May we have your key to the apartment? I don't have it."

He fished in a shirt pocket, and gave her a key. "Garage's open," he said. "You'll find everything shipshape, Miz Palmer."

"I'm sure of it," she told him. They went across to the garage while Mr. Jackson looked after them thoughtfully. He wondered if she'd bring it off. He hoped so. He liked Katie Palmer. How she manages to be friendly and cheerful working for that shrewd old bitch, he thought, is beyond me. But Mrs. Warner had picked him for this job, a good one; didn't take too much of his time, and he'd grown rather attached to the place. If this fella buys it, he thought, maybe he'd have me around full time. Of course if he has a wife, there could be a hitch. Women usually hate people their husbands hire. But he don't look married to me.

Two-car garage, a workshop, and stairs going up. The apartment was, as Katie had said, attractive: a big living room, a good-sized bedroom and a bath, well furnished, not in antiques but in good reproductions. At the end of the living room the narrow kitchen, range, sink—rather like a galley with shelves, cupboards and a counter, and Katie said, "This apartment is heated, from the garage, by oil. Living room and bedroom have window air conditioners. As you see, it's pretty complete."

"Hey," said Cam, and sat down on the single bed, "come sit awhile."

She said, sitting beside him, "It would do for guests, you know."

"Wait a minute. . . . How much does he want for the place, furniture included?"

Her heart sank like a little stone in cold unfriendly waters. She said, "Well, the asking price . . ."

"Is what?"

She told him. He whistled. "Mortgage?" he asked.

"Yes." She told him the amount and he thought for a moment. Then he lit a cigarette, and Katie handed him the ashtray from the bedside table.

"Will he come down?" Cam inquired.

"I think so."

"Find out how much. I'll assume the mortgage and pay him cash."

Katie's heart now floated to a warmer and sunny surface. She said, "You really like it, Cam?"

"It's almost exactly what I want—not, of course, at his so-called asking price. Can you get in touch with Mrs. Warner?"

"I'll phone and leave messages. Yes, of course."

"And she can reach Andrews?"

"She has several phone numbers . . . there's the time difference, of course, but she'll reach him by phone. She can also cable."

"Okay, let's go. I have to get back to the city, I've an engagement, but I can come out Monday and talk to your Mrs. Warner . . . if we can get things under way."

On the way out he stopped in the patio. Mr. Jackson was sitting on an old stool, leaning against the wall and about to eat his lunch. "Well, Mr. Jackson, I'm making an offer for the house and if it's accepted, I'll see you around," Cam told him.

Mr. Jackson dropped his sandwich. He said inadequately, "Sure. That'll be fine."

"Do you always make up your mind so fast?" asked Katie as they got into the car.

"Sure. Why not?"

"On everything?"

"Almost. Women—sometimes too fast there. Horses— I'm usually lucky. Cars, houses, colors. . . . Think he'll take the offer?"

"I'm almost sure of it."

"I forgot to ask about property taxes."

She could quote him that figure too. He said resignedly, "Well, okay. . . . how'd you like me for a neighbor?"

"Just fine. Jeremy, too."

"Sometimes I wish Jeremy and I had been in a shooting war," he remarked idly.

"Why, for heaven's sake?"

"He was always rescuing me," Cam told her, "from one situation or another. I never had to rescue him. In a shooting war I would have, Katie. Didn't you know he's reckless—

or would be in a dangerous situation? Otherwise, not. Me, I'm the other side of the coin, reckless when it comes to ordinary situations—women, money—mine, not someone else's—but I'd be cautious if the bullets flew. However, I'm also the heroic type," he said complacently. "I'd have dragged old Jeremy into whatever was handy, trench, underbrush . . ." He grinned. "Come back to the Inn and lunch with me, Jeremy too," he said.

"I'll take you there, Cam, but I have to go to the office and get things moving. I'll see if Jeremy's free. We'll join you."

She dropped Cam off, went back to the office and miraculously found a parking space. She dashed in, said wildly to Flo, "I think he'll buy it. . . . You've Mrs. Warner's hotel number?"

"Yes," said Flo, astonished, "but——"

"Never mind the buts, start phoning and paging—maybe if she went out to lunch she's left word where she'll be. I'll be at the Inn for an hour and then at home."

She hurried out, down the street and into the bookshop, which was crowded. She asked Mary Hawes, "Where's Jeremy?" and Mrs. Hawes indicated that he was in his small office. Katie went in, and Jeremy was standing by his desk in the midst of clutter—the state of his office always astonished her—talking to a young woman with red hair who if she wasn't utterly beautiful, need not lose any sleep over it. He looked up, startled. "Katie," he said, and then, "This is my wife, Beth. Katie—Beth Nelson."

Katie shook hands, her eyes registering the fact that Mrs. Nelson was a dazzler, but her mind otherwise occupied. She said, "Jeremy, I think Cam's going to buy the house. He wants us to come to lunch at the Inn. . . . he's there now."

"You go," said Jeremy. "I can't leave. Tell him he's crazy, will you? But I'm glad." He moved toward her and kissed her, said, "See you later," and seemingly dismissed her.

Katie drove back to the Inn, where Cam was waiting in the cocktail lounge. He asked, "Where's Jeremy?"

He's busy. Says you're insane, but he's glad." She sat down and he asked, "What'll you have, after you've caught your breath?"

"Usually I don't have anything at midday—but this could be a celebration." She ordered a Bloody Mary, and said, "I don't believe it."

"Believe it . . . if Andrews accepts the offer."

"If he does, when would you move in?"

"Oh, around Christmas. I've things to do. I had a good offer for my apartment, not long ago. I'll take it. And I want to lease a small one for the nights I'll have to spend in town."

"What about furniture?" asked Katie practically.

"I'll take out enough for the humble pad," he told her, "and a very few personal things. I've never become attached to furnishings. I move in, hang up my hat, move out. One of the things that was wrong with my marriage was Sybil's inability to do just that—not that I blame her. Women are like cats." He added, "I see Ronnie during her Christmas holidays. This Christmas she can spend most of her free time with me. . . . What about Mr. Jackson?"

"What about him?" Katie asked bewildered.

"Doesn't he have a given name?"

"If so, I never knew it," Katie answered.

"I like him. Think he'd work for me? Looks strong as a horse, though I daresay he's on Social Security. He could take care of the outside work."

Having finished their drinks they went in to lunch, during which Cam produced a card and wrote on it. He said, "You can get me at the apartment, my club, or through my answering service. Let me know if anything moves over the weekend. Tell Mrs. Warner if it does, I'll be at her office at ten on Monday. We can talk terms, lawyers, references, banks." He grinned, and added simply, "I hate wasting time. There's damned little of it, really."

Afterwards he walked Katie to her car, opened the door, kissed her firmly, and said, "See you Monday, and thanks."

"Cam . . . what about help, aside from Mr. Jackson?"

"Don't fret. I have a superb housekeeper. Sybil and I almost came to blows over Mrs. Latimer. I'm the only one allowed to call her Polly. But I had her first. Stole her from my brother and his wife. She never liked my brother. The garage apartment will be fine for her, and she likes the country. She came originally from up here somewhere. As for the rest, she'll hire people as she needs them. Now, be off. I have to pay my bill and get back to town and do a little arithmetic."

8

✳✳✳✳ When Jeremy came home, it was raining a little, a small disconsolate drizzle. He put Katie's car away and let himself in the back door. He heard Katie talking to someone upstairs. Phone, he concluded, as he saw no evidence of visitors. He ascended the stairs, two steps at a time.

Katie hung up as he came in. Her small face was flushed, her hair in becoming disarray, as if she'd been running her hands through it, as indeed she had. She bounced up from the bed where she'd been sitting and into his arms. "That was Cam. . . . Isn't it marvelous?"

"Yes. Quite so. Simmer down." He walked her back to the bed, sat her down on it, and stood over her, his hands in his pockets.

"Jeremy, don't loom!" She added distractedly. "I haven't done a thing about dinner."

He sat down beside her and remarked, "I was sure you hadn't. I'll cope, or we can walk over to the seafood place after we've had a drink—whichever you say."

"It's raining. I don't want to walk anywhere."

"Then I'll get out the car."

"Scrambled eggs here," she said. "Coffee—that would be fine."

"What did you have for lunch?"

"A souffle and salad. . . . Why?"

"I had milk and a sandwich, in the shop. I'll get us some sort of nourishment. Brush your hair. Do a little Yoga. Contemplate your delightful navel, then join me in a drink."

"Jeremy, don't you want to hear all about it?"

"Of course, in due time. But not from a young, pretty, or euphoric Witch of Endor. Take a number of deep breaths. I'll be waiting with the aperitif, after looking in the freezer."

"But I want to talk now!"

"It will keep. If you talk now, you'll babble."

He further disordered her hair, went out of the room and shut the door. Katie lay back on the bed. She thought: Someday I'll cut his throat. This monumental calm.

When she went downstairs, having changed and remedied her hair and lipstick, Jeremy was in the study. "Fat, good rare hamburgers," he said, "in case you're interested, the little peas you like, creamed celery."

"I hate creamed celery."

"I don't. And fruit and cheese for dessert." He poured her drink, gestured toward a plate of crackers, and lifted his own glass.

"To your success and Cam's contentment," he said. "Now, tell me what you've been up to all day."

She said, "He made up his mind almost at once, quoted a price, and said he'd like to hire Mr. Jackson."

"Who in—oh, sure, the quaint caretaker. . . . And then?"

"I left word with Flo to get hold of Mrs. Warner, who called me here, an hour after I got home. The appointment's set up for Cam here at ten on Monday. By then she will have run Andrews to earth. Cam said he'd assume the mortgage and pay Andrews in cash . . . right on the barrel-head."

"He has it," said her husband, "and he's a shrewder operator than most people—except, of course, his customers—give him credit for. Did your formidable Emily think Andrews would take the offer?"

"Yes. She's always known how far down he'd come—she's never told me, however." She looked at him and laughed. "It will be great fun," she predicted, "having Cam in Little Oxford."

"Very like throwing a match into a nest of fireworks," he agreed. "But I enjoy fireworks—from a safe distance. What's he going to do with the penthouse apartment?"

"It's a penthouse? He's going to sell it, take a small flat for when he has to stay in town. He had it all worked out in his mind in case he liked the Andrews house or any other. He says he always moves fast. Does he?"

"Speed of light," Jeremy agreed. "When's he moving in, by the way?"

"Sometime before Christmas. Of course he'll be up in between. Did you know he knows Mrs. William Niles?"

"No. She's nice to know, however. I like her."

"Jeremy, you never told me you knew her!"

"You never asked and I haven't seen her since before we were married. I met her at Jessica's and she'd pop into the shop now and then. She's a good customer when she isn't somewhere else. Where did Cam run into her?"

"Paris. . . . He's bringing his cook here."

"Rosie Niles?"

"Do you call her Rosie? Of course not, idiot, his cook, whatever her name is."

"Mrs. Latimer," said Jeremy. "Wonder if you could arrange for her to give you a few lessons."

"You know her too."

"I," said Jeremy grandly, "know practically everybody."

"But you never talk about them."

"Now why should I talk about Rosie or Cam's housekeeper, unless in some mysterious way their names enter a conversation?"

"I don't know, but it's one of your most infuriating habits."

He said, "The reason I have friends and acquaintances is that I don't talk about them superfluously."

Katie held out her glass. She said, "You drive me to it—I'll have half a refill."

He obliged and said, "When I finish mine, I'll turn chef. Will you be strong enough to set the table?"

"By then yes, or else flat on my face. Your Beth Nelson is lovely. Cam was right."

"She's not mine," he said sadly. "Why does everyone assume it? I just employ the girl. And to answer the question you haven't asked yet, yes, I like her; she's pleasant to have around. And looking into my crystal ball I predict that Cam will become a permanent paying customer, if only for coffee-table books—the large, illustrated, expensive ones. They are after all, the jam on my bread and butter, so, I'm hoping."

He rose, kissed her and said, "I'm glad you had a good day, darling; and don't start fretting about that call to Paris. Emily will get through floods, earthquakes and hurricanes. She'll probably call you at three tomorrow morning, or thereabouts, damn her. But if you stew while waiting, you'll ruin your digestion, which could have an unhappy effect upon your skin. I'm off. Sit there, finish your drink, and think peacefully about your eventual commission. All these little wrinkles will be ironed out. Rest your small carcass, just drag it out in time to set the table. Man's work," added Jeremy mournfully, "is never done."

Lying back on the couch, relaxed and smiling, Katie thought: Even when he maddens me, he's wonderful.

After supper and washing up, Jeremy asked, "How about Scrabble? Music?"

Katie shook her head and he said, resigned, "Okay, but let's try a little something to take your grasshopper mind off Emily's inevitable, programmed telephone call. . . . Don't look so startled; I'm not propositioning you, it's too soon after our quite inspired dinner. Suppose we join the majority of those happy mindless people and watch TV? I sometimes enjoy the commercials."

The television set was in the living room. They watched comfortably, a documentary on ecology and then a remarkably good mystery filled with humor, creeps, near disasters, a murder or two and an endless racing of cars through a stormy night. Katie, as usual, kept up a running commentary, something she sometimes did even in a motion-picture theater. But, here, there was no one to hiss, "Will you please be quiet?" at her.

After the late news they went upstairs, and to bed and at about five o'clock on Sunday morning the telephone rang.

Jeremy sat up, switched on his light and picked up the instrument, saying "Hell's bells!" to no one in particular. And Katie roused herself, crying, "It has to be for me."

"It certainly has to," he agreed, handed her the phone and lay back listening to her exclamations: "You did? . . . But that's wonderful! . . . No, of course, I wasn't asleep. I've been awake all night, waiting."

And finally: "Yes. Ten o'clock tomorrow."

She returned the telephone to her husband and said, "She reached Mr. Andrews just a few minutes ago."

"Too soon," Jeremy commented. "I take it he's agreeable to the offer?"

"Oh, yes. . . . At first he wasn't—for about two expensive minutes," she said. "She's been calling him all night. I still don't understand the time difference."

"Five hours. . . . No, not now. . . . France is on permanent daylight saving, and we aren't yet."

"He'd just gotten home," said Katie. "Give me the phone again, Jeremy."

"Not so fast, I don't advise you to call Cam at this hour. If he's asleep and you wake him, he'll cancel the deal; or if he's just getting in, he'll be equally enraged. Wait until about nine. He'll be up or at least viable by then. So you go on back to sleep or if you're too excited to do so, come over here and I'll tell you a sort of bedtime story." He drew her close and added, "Not every man has a crazy little woman for a wife, but then, not all men are as fortunate as I am."

At nine, after breakfast, Katie called Cam and told him the news and Cam unruffled, said, "Well, good. See you tomorrow at the office. Congratulations to all of us—you, me, Mr. Andrews. Give Jeremy my best—no, let me speak to him."

Jeremy took the phone and Cam said, "Sorry about this, but there goes your neighborhood."

When he hung up, smiling, Katie said, "I don't think Cam was alone."

"Why?"

"Oh, I heard flutters and such in the background, even, perhaps, a girlish giggle."

Jeremy said reproachfully, "Now and then his paternal

grandmother comes on from Boston and stays with him. Nice old gal, quite deaf and close to ninety."

"And what," inquired Katie, "does his housekeeper think about that?"

"She isn't paid to think about Cam's life style. Polly Latimer cooks up a storm, rules Cam's household, loves him and his child, hates his ex-wife, feels guilty about being swiped from his brother's kitchen and ignores her employer's masculine weaknesses. She'll have your head with dumplings for dinner if you venture to criticize his slightest move in any direction."

"Is she young and beautiful?" Katie asked, yawning. She felt relaxed, almost let down, the crisis having passed successfully.

"No. She was eighteen, I think she told me, when she went to work for Cam's parents. By the time Cam was in the service, his elder brother had married and she went with them. The older Rosses had taken up travel, or when they were in this country a hotel suite in Florida in winter; in summer, Long Island—the place where Cam grew up and which was a wedding gift to his brother. Polly Latimer is elderly, healthy, strong and dynamic, and she'll work for Cam until she drops or he retires her on a very good pension. That is, unless he remarries, and it's someone she doesn't like. She and Sybil fought like amazons, yet Sybil wanted her included in the divorce settlement. There's absolutely no one like her. I'm terrified of her, frankly."

"I wonder if she'll like me."

"Of course, unless you have designs on her boss."

"I'll tell her I haven't."

"She'll see for herself," said Jeremy. "I'm going to walk up and get the papers. What time are we due at Linda's?"

"She said six or thereabouts."

"We'll make it thereabouts," Jeremy decided.

It was a little after the hour when they reached the small town of Deeport in which Linda and Tom Davis lived. They had half an acre and a small tidy house, set back from a quiet street. Tom came out on the porch to meet them. He was stocky, fair, with candid blue eyes and a shrewd, composed mouth, now widened to a grin. He said exactly what his guests had expected, as he always said it: "Long time no see." He talked, Jeremy had once remarked, in stereotype. "Rather endearing," he'd added, "and so predictable it's nostalgic."

They went in, shed their outdoor attire and Linda romped into the small square hall. "Hi," she said, and patted her flawless front, "meet the expectant Mama."

They kissed her and Jeremy then held her at arm's length admiringly. "No one would guess it," he told her and Linda exposed a dimple in her left cheek. She was as pretty as a dessert in a magazine advertisement—also small, quick and vivacious. Katie was fond of Linda; she was, beneath the urchin curls, a solid citizen, endowed with uncommon common sense, practical and honest. Shortly before Linda's marriage, Katie had asked her, "Are you sure about this, Linda? You and Tom have been splitting and going back together again ever since I've known you." And Linda had answered, "Well, it isn't as if I hadn't been living with him off and on; I know what I'm getting, Katie, and it's better than anything else I've been offered. We'll fight like crazy just as we have since we were kids, but Tom needs shaking up every so often. Being with Tom's rather like wearing comfortable old shoes. Now and then your feet itch and you kick them off. New shoes are something else, no matter how good they look in the display case or when the salesman fits them."

Over drinks, served lavishly with elegant little hot and cold appetizers, Tom asked, "What do you think of our starting a family?"

Jeremy said, "Marvelous," and Katie answered, "Well, great if you planned it."

Linda said, "We hadn't—not for another year."

And Tom remarked, "Try it, you'll like it." He added, "She doesn't upchuck mornings—at least not yet—but I do."

"Only here at home," Linda hastened to reassure them, "never at the bank. Personally I think he's read a book about expectant fathers and is just showing off, or else," she added thoughtfully, "it's the new toothpaste."

Tom regarded his wife with what Jeremy had once called "the little woman look." He said, "We're going to attend classes at the hospital together. Natural childbirth, you know."

For the rest of the evening he hovered, bearing trays, opening doors, carrying dishes out and Linda said resignedly, "Don't worry, folks, this solicitude will wear off, my doctor promised, in a couple of weeks or so. Actually, I don't think Tom will last through the delivery room."

"What about your job?" Katie asked her.

Linda, since her marriage, had worked in her oldest brother's law office. "Oh, I'll work until I can't get through the door, I suppose," she answered.

Tom said firmly, "She doesn't have to. I keep telling her that."

"I'm not sitting at home knitting little garments," Linda said firmly. "I can't knit. Neither am I trekking around, exchanging girl talk with pregnant friends, or listening to others telling me about their terrible ordeals. I'd be bored to death, as well as scared. I've already heard a few of them talk."

On the way home, Katie was silent until they turned their corner, and then she said, "Tom's really impossible. Beaming like a full moon. Morning sickness, for heaven's sake!"

"It's not unusual."

"Poor Linda! She has to hold his head and carry the baby too. You'd think he was going to have it."

"In general," Jeremy told her, "men are the romanticists, and women, practical, however sentimental."

"Instant analysis," said Katie. "I don't envy Linda."

"Of course not," he agreed. "On the other hand, she doesn't envy you. Linda's amusing, Katie. I always enjoyed her and you enjoy Tom. After dinner, I watched you and our host talking about tight money, loans, mortgages, the rise and fall of real estate. You were having a ball. Don't put him down."

"Oh, I don't. He's very sound," Katie admitted, "but now and then he'd stop talking shop long enough to invite my praise for his achievement."

"I daresay that he did have something to do with it."

"A simple, biological act," Katie reminded him, "but Linda will carry the burden of the consequences quite literally."

"Also, a simple biological act," Jeremy told her, laughing. "They're both fine, and, as far as I could tell, happy. Tom's delighted and so is Linda. He'll go on getting raises at the bank and squirreling money away; kids cost a lot, I understand."

"Just the same," Katie said, "I wish they'd waited another year or two."

"My little love," said Jeremy, "marriage is not an obsolete institution, despite those who proclaim so. Given certain requirements—which I think Linda and Tom have—it's still a His and Her arrangement; or should I say, Her and His?"

Katie rolled up her window and he asked, "What's the matter, are you cold?"

"There's a nasty little wind," Katie answered, "and winter's not far away. It won't be long before we return to standard time. I wish we had daylight saving year round."

"So," said Jeremy, "the autumnal fires will soon be banked. Never mind. It looks like an exciting season ahead, and besides, I promise, in any weather, to keep you warm!"

9

✳✳✳✳ November came in, mild and gray, with high winds, and blowing rain. Most of the trees were bare, save for a few stubborn leaves which held to their fading colors; but the oak leaves remained as others fell. Katie thought that the most remarkable thing about that autumn was the way Cam and Emily got along which was evident to her from their first meeting. She spoke of this to Jeremy and he said, "I suspect that they respect—and even understand—each other. And Cam, despite any disclaimer you may have heard him make, can be as cautious as your Emily."

Cam came and went, staying at the Inn and seeing Katie and Jeremy frequently. During this period Katie grew to know Veronica, a short, chunky child. "My doctor says it's puppy fat," she explained to Katie. "I got scared, sort of, and went on a crash diet. Wow! Anyway he promised me I'll slim down." She had big, slate-colored eyes, flyaway fair hair, and good features. Katie found her outrageous, funny, too advanced but endearing. Ronnie was madly in love with

Jeremy, she informed them both, "not that I wasn't before this—when I was just a child."

"What a kid!" Katie remarked to her husband later. "But then I haven't had much to do with nine-year-olds."

"She's very bright," Jeremy told her, "and, I deduce, torn between her father, whom she loves, and her mother for whom she appears to have a curious maternal concern."

"At nine? You've lost me," Katie said.

Cam's Mrs. Latimer came also, numerous times. Katie had offered the guest room, but Mrs. Latimer declined. Too much coming and going, she said. She couldn't impose. The Inn was the solution. The first time she came to Little Oxford it was with her employer and Ronnie, over a weekend. Ronnie and Cam had dinner with the Palmers but not Mrs. Latimer. Katie had asked them all, by telephone. Before dinner, she asked, "Did you tell her I can't cook? You needn't have bothered, Jeremy's doing most of it tonight."

"No. Polly's a snob. She has a fixation about what's her place and what isn't. Everyone else's too. When we're settled in Little Oxford and you run over to see that nothing leaks or whatever, she'll ask you to have tea with her in the kitchen—or her living room. Someday you may be able to coax her to have a cup with you here on Baker street. Her family was in service for generations; her mother wound up as head housekeeper to a belted Lord. Polly came here from England when she was eighteen. The Castle was then on the tourist tour, and she couldn't take that. She has relatives in the States and as you know, was first with my parents, then with my brother."

"But what about her husband? Did she marry in England or here?"

"She's never married. When you're a tweeny, a house, or parlor maid, you'd be Polly—in her case. But a housekeeper gets the courtesy title, so once she'd advanced in my parents' household, she became Mrs. Latimer. At that time the compromise hadn't been invented."

Mrs. Latimer, of course, met Mr. Jackson, and Cam reported that they eyed each other like fighters, each from his corner and stepped out warily. But he thought they approved, each of the other.

When Mrs. Latimer invaded Little Oxford alone, she drove a compact, competently, and always saw Katie, and sometimes Emily Warner, in order to familiarize herself with the domestic-by-day situation, the village and the shops. She was a tall woman, on the gaunt side, with small brilliant blue eyes, pepper-and-salt hair, and, Jeremy said, a truly Gothic face.

The first light snow fell just before Thanksgiving on which day Katie and Jeremy went to the Bankses for the festivities. One of their daughters and her new husband were there; the older Irvingtons dropped by toward evening with Letty's quiet delightful father; and the young Irvingtons came too, complete with baby. Others came and went. Jessica had plenty of help, and there was a moveable-feast buffet if you came for late supper, sit-down if at four o'clock.

It was a good day, but at the end of it Katie was very tired; in fact, she was at the end of every day. It had been a busy season in the office, a good deal of selling, and almost as much buying before winter iced them in. Katie had finally sold the Grantson property to people with the means to restore it and a large, young family which would probably unrestore it in a few years. But being exhausted was not like Katie. "You look like hell in a hand basket," Emily commented. "You're not pregnant, are you?"

"God forbid," Katie answered in pious horror.

"I hope not," Emily told her. "I can't spare you for long and I doubt God has anything to do with pregnancy."

Finally at Jeremy's insistence, Katie went to see Ben Irvington.

He didn't keep her waiting long. She had just time to chat briefly with Elvira Jones, his father's incomparable nurse, whom Ben shared.

"What's wrong, Katie?" he asked.

"I don't know. You're the doctor. Nothing, I guess, but I'm so tired I could die. The thought of Christmas fills me with terror. I barely made it through Thanksgiving. And if I'm pregnant, I'll kill myself!"

The checkup took an hour and a half. When it was over and she was dressed and sitting at the desk again, Ben said, "You're not pregnant—which is a pity, sort of—I like babies. You're fine, Katie, except for what appears to be nervous exhaustion . . . overdoing, driving yourself."

"It will let up at the office; it already has," she said quickly.

"Okay, that's good. However, you're to rest more. I'll give you something to relax you and something to build you up. You're young and basically healthy, but you could be young and unhealthy too. I want you to eat and sleep properly and have fun—not just going out to dinner now and then, but trying to enjoy yourself. In your present state I'm sure you don't enjoy anything, not even Jeremy, or selling a house."

Katie said after a moment, "I know. I get irritated. I feel raw, and itchy, and I snap at people. Of course, one just doesn't snap at Mrs. Warner and it kills me not to——"

"Do you cry when you're alone?"

"Sometimes," she admitted, "and I'm not a weeper by nature."

"I suppose Jeremy knows?"

"I don't cry on his shoulder if that's what you mean, but

he'd seriously doubt that I got mascara in my eyes or had been peeling onions. I hadn't said anything, but he made me come see you."

"Made you? How reactionary."

"Well, if I hadn't, he would have nagged—gently, of course, but, still nagged."

"And you resent that?"

"I don't like to be treated as if I were a retarded child. I can look after myself, and have ever since I was, maybe, ten. You know my mother—all sorts of preoccupations and projects. And my father was always preoccupied with her. . . . I know I'm not ill, Ben, just tired."

"It isn't physical fatigue, Katie. You're still adjusting to losing your—shall we call it independence? You and Jeremy haven't been married long; you're still on the shakedown cruise; Jeremy, too." He smiled, his special warm smile. "But human nature being what it is, you'd resent it if Jeremy *didn't* worry about you. Tell him to come see me."

"He's perfectly well," Katie informed him, "and I don't want or need a family consultation."

"Very well. . . . Have the prescriptions filled. I'll check and if you haven't, it will be my turn to nag."

The telephone rang and he answered, saying, "Yes, Nuisance. . . . No. I'm not involved with anything serious. Katie's here. Want to speak to her for three minutes? Patients are impatiently awaiting. Elvira is trying to entertain them."

"Amy," he reported unnecessarily and gave Katie the instrument. "I'll call her back," he said.

In less than three minutes she'd replaced the telephone, gathered up her prescriptions and risen. Ben took her to the door. "Thanks, Ben," she said.

"You don't mean it. Next time you feel like crying try Jeremy's shoulder on for size."

Out in the gray late afternoon, Katie looked at her watch. She could stop in at the office.

A car pulled away from the curb near the building. Katie parked and went in. As she entered the reception room Emily emerged into it, from her office. She said, "Didn't expect you back today. Come in and talk to me for a minute. You've seen Ben?"

"Yes," Katie answered. "I didn't tell you where I was going. Who's the spy in Baker Street? Or is the place bugged?"

"No. You are obvious. Anyway you left his number with Flo in case there was a call for you from Mrs. Jason. There wasn't."

Katie wandered into Mrs. Warner's quarters and sat down.

"You're pregnant," Emily predicted, sighing.

"No, of course not," Katie said crossly.

"Good. . . . Then what is the matter with you?"

"Ben said I'm overdoing, that I drive myself."

Emily responded unsympathetically, "Everyone does; we all go through pressures and tensions. Relax. Mrs. Jason will either buy the Willis cottage or she won't. There'll be others like her. Things are beginning to slow up. I'm planning a cruise in January or February; nothing settled yet. Run along home now. See you tomorrow."

The phone rang as Katie let herself in. It was Jeremy, asking, "What did Ben say?"

"Very little. Just that I was overdoing; gave me some advice and a couple of prescriptions. Made me feel neurotic."

"Aren't we all? . . . Look, I forgot about the Chamber of Commerce dinner until about an hour ago. I'll cancel out and come home. Unless you'll change your mind and go with me."

"The dinner chairman would have a stroke at this late

hour. Don't be silly. A cancellation isn't a disaster, but an unexpected guest is. Besides, I have a date."

"With whom?"

"Amy Irvington. I talked to her from Ben's office. She'll park the infant with the grandparents and run over to see me. Ben's going to a meeting after dinner."

"I'll be home to change and also to see that you get something to eat. I'll bring a casserole."

Katie hung up, shook her head to clear her eyes and swallowed the obstruction in her throat. Jeremy's solicitude both touched and annoyed her. In her mind she called it "hovering." He'd worried about her before, but she never knew—and didn't now—how much was serious, how much, not. He hovered, and darted away, cheerfully. Going upstairs to renew her face she thought: Damnit, I forgot to stop and leave the prescriptions, well, I'll do it tomorrow. And thought further: I simply don't *know* him, or myself either. Who am I anyway?

She was glad Amy was coming; she could talk to Amy. Not that she ever had, really. But they were almost the same age, if not in the same situation. Amy didn't work now; and she'd never had an exacting selling, pleasing everyone sort of job; also she had a baby. Linda? Linda was completely absorbed in her loving, running battles with Tom and her new pregnancy.

No one is really like anyone else, thought Katie desolately.

She put her outdoor things in the hall closet and went into the living room. Jeremy had brought a new novel home. Katie lay down on the couch, picked it up, looked at a page in the beginning, then at a few more, and put it aside. Same old thing, ethnics, sex, the usual words, a touch of violence, war . . .

She heard Jeremy at the back door. Then he came loping

in, a basket in his hand, covered with a red and white cloth. "Casserole," he said. "Also a salad and a pint of the red wine you like. . . . You all right?"

"I'm fine."

He walked into the kitchen, came back and leaned down to kiss her. "All you have to do is put the casserole in a slow oven for approximately ten minutes. Wine's room temperature, salad's tossed," he said.

He'd been to The Checked Tablecloth, which made casseroles, appetizers, salads, and other delicacies for the weary housewife.

Now he sat down on the couch and demanded, "Tell me everything Ben said from the moment you walked into his office."

She complied, imparting most of it; what she omitted was strictly her business.

"I wish you'd quit Warner's, Katie."

"I know. But I don't want to; I'd crawl the walls with boredom." She added, "Mrs. Warner is taking a cruise this winter. I wish we could get away over Christmas."

"You know that's my busiest time, Katie. Maybe later, if things are running smoothly, we can take a week in Florida."

"A week isn't time enough to get used to the change of climate. Anyway I dread Christmas. You're always late getting home, and I have to struggle with the Christmas list and address the cards too."

"It will give you something to do, as it did last year. And you've done half the cards already." He laughed, made a long arm and pulled her to him. "Just don't try to do too much. . . . Is your mother coming down?"

"She hasn't said so. But we're asked to Cam's."

"If she comes, Cam will be delighted. He'll love her." He

rose. "Have to change," he said. "I'll be home early. Did you leave your prescriptions at Lowell's?"

"I'll do that tomorrow."

"Where are they? I'll give them to Wes."

"In my handbag on the chair. But the pharmacy will be closed."

"Wes Lowell will be at the dinner."

He found the prescriptions, went upstairs and was down again in no time flat. "I'll put the casserole in the oven and set the timer," he told her. "When it goes off, retrieve your dinner and eat it." He kissed her and left.

Katie took a transistor into the kitchen, found some music, set a place at the little table, opened the wine, transferred the salad to a bowl and when the timer rang, seized a pair of potholders. She carried the casserole to the table and put it on a trivet. She wasn't hungry of course . . . but everything was delicious. She ate, music around her and another book beside her, a good fast romantic mystery.

Katie had finished washing up and was back on the couch, reading Mrs. Eberhart's latest when someone came up the front steps and smartly whacked the door. "Anyone in?" asked Amy.

"It's not locked," called Katie, and got there as Amy entered, rosy and wrapped in fake fur. "Did you know it's snowing?" she inquired.

"No. Throw your coat somewhere and come on in. I wish I'd asked you to supper. Jeremy—via The Checked Tablecloth—provided me with a casserole and salad and also brought me some fancy wine."

"How can he afford it?" Amy inquired. "It's cold out," she added.

"We can sit in the study, it's warmer."

"Nope. Fine here. I couldn't have come to supper. I had to feed Ben before his meeting, he's always ravenous. He says, 'Don't bother, woman, I'm not hungry,' and then proceeds to eat as if emerging from hibernation."

"Did he call you back?"

"Who? Oh, Ben. Of course, between patients."

"Did he say anything about me?"

"Wouldn't be ethical," said Amy solemnly. "Of course I guessed from his tone that you have a dread disease. May I perch?"

Katie said, "Yes. Put your feet up. Want a sherry or something?"

"No, thanks. Are you going to tell Mama what's wrong with you?"

"Is that ethical?" pondered Katie aloud. "Actually nothing. Overtired, is all."

"I forgot. Before Ben left the house and I took off for the aging parents', he said to tell you he expected you to have the prescriptions filled. Did you?"

"No and yes."

"Get it all together."

"Of course you understand that if I don't take one capsule every eleven minutes, I'll die on a Tuesday at six," Katie said.

"A.M. or P.M.? . . . Don't answer that. . . . How come no and yes?"

"No, I forgot and yes, Jeremy took them to Wes Lowell, who is at the dinner tonight."

"That clears up everything. Why are you tired?"

"A good question. It's been a very busy season at the Warner we-sell-everything-we-can-lay-our hands on."

"But it's slackening."

"That's right, thank God."

"You're not really grateful, you're wondering how bored you'll become by midwinter."

"I suppose you're right," said Katie mildly.

Amy sat up on her end of the couch and put her arms

around her knees. She was, thought Katie, such a pretty woman.

"I know what's bugging you," Amy said. "You've got the 'I love him but why in hell did I ever get married?' blues."

Katie said, astonished, "Thank you, doctor. It sounds ridiculous."

"It isn't. Most every female experiences the 'what am I doing in this situation?' fatigue."

"But I haven't been married long enough!" Katie wailed.

"It can happen in a week or less. You know Ben's grandparents gave Ben and me a trip to France as a wedding gift? They had a rental car waiting at the plane and we were to drive to them, stopping along the way. At a hotel in the last town before theirs Ben got sick. He was furiously diagnosing himself. I was trying to cope with the telephone in order to get a doctor. My high school French! I was frantic. He had a roaring temperature and his disposition was horrible. I got the doctor, but I couldn't understand a word he said and Ben, I think, even less. I managed somehow to get Granny on the phone and she and Grandpa drove that last fifty miles to cope. In the interim I wished to heaven I'd never married. I blamed Ben, of course, because I'd wanted to go on to the Lovemans' and he wanted to spend the night on the road. . . . Well, there have been times since."

Katie asked fascinated, "How and why?"

"I've been married longer than you, Katie, but I assure you it's no bed of roses. I'm sure you've found that out. Ben's mother warned me that being a doctor's wife was no sinecure. It wasn't and isn't. Besides, I missed working. You and Jeremy will make it to number fifty, as I know Ben and I will."

"I thought the danger point was the seventh year," said

Katie, "and so I planned somehow to skip it and go on to the eighth."

"Every year," said Amy firmly, "you're building something The plans get lost or you find you haven't put in a window, or the roof falls in." She laughed. "I try to understand everything Ben tells me about his work—which isn't much. I even consult Elvira, Letty and Bing, and read horrifying medical books. After all I had a faint smattering, having worked in the hospital. Thank heaven Benjy isn't old enough yet to cause dissension over how to bring him up, although Ben's beginning to fret over what he feels is a lack of discipline. He says I'm permissive!"

Katie said, "Jeremy and I don't—well I hate the word; it's on every radio and TV show, in every kind of print—it's communicate."

"Did you expect to, in a couple of years? It takes twenty, at least, and sometimes people never achieve it."

Katie said hesitantly, "There's nothing wrong with our basic relationship."

"Of course not. You and Jeremy are lucky. Ben and I too."

"Jeremy's completely immersed in books," said Katie, "and I suppose the real estate business has me hooked. I don't know much about books, and he couldn't care less about real estate."

"You'll learn, and maybe he will. I'm not sure, but I think the burden of learning is on the female. Men," said Amy, "are wonderful, but they rarely learn anything outside of their own interests. Keep your chin up and try not to lead with it. This too will pass until the next time," she added.

She left in an hour or so. Katie went to bed, listened to the radio and for Jeremy.

Her prescriptions were delivered to the office the next

morning. She took them dutifully, became interested in the problems of a young couple looking for a small house they couldn't quite afford and then, about two weeks before Christmas, with her gift list attended to, reached home before Jeremy on a dark afternoon. Walking up the back steps, exasperated because she hadn't left the light on, she skidded on a small skim of glacéd snow, clutched wildly at the air, fell over Lancelot and ruined a perfectly good ankle.

10

✳✳✳✳ Lancelot barked, Katie swore, the Elder twins, returning from band practice, came tearing up the steps. "You hurt?" Doug yelled and Jim pushed Lancelot down the steps and said anxiously, "Gosh, that dog!"

"Ice," said Katie, trying to struggle up. The twins helped, each crying, "Lean on me," and Katie somehow got to her feet and held fast to Doug. "My ankle," she said. "Jim, get the key from my handbag and open the door."

Olive, hearing the commotion, steamed out on her porch and across. "What happened?" she asked as, with the door open, Doug and Jim were endeavoring to convoy Katie inside, and Katie was emitting little yelps.

"Carry her," Olive counseled. "She doesn't weigh more than a football. There. For heaven's sake, get some lights on. On the couch, boys. Be careful. If Katie fell over your dinosaur, your father will shoot us all."

"Just ice," said Katie. "Lancelot was there, and I fell over him, but not before I'd slipped and twisted my ankle."

Olive said, "I'll get your shoe off and call Ben Irvington."

"Jeremy first," said Katie, in a dying voice. "He can take me to the hospital or office or someplace . . . probably the dump."

"What's the number?"

Katie told her. Doug brought her a glass of water, which he spilled, and Lancelot howled dismally in the darkness outside.

Olive dialed and held a short conversation. "Someone says Jeremy's gone out on an errand with someone named Nelson," she reported.

"Nelson," repeated Katie, electrified. Then, "So call Ben —I'll talk to him."

Ben was out on a house call, but Elvira was still at the office. She said, "I'll get hold of him, Katie. Can someone bring you to the office? He'll want an X ray. I'll stay on."

Katie hung up. "Office," she said and Olive nodding, "I'll drive you. The boys will help me get you in your car."

"She probably needs an ambulance," said Doug who had watched many a medical TV show.

"I'll get your bedroom slippers," said Olive. "Where are they?"

"Look on a chair or under the bed. I still have one good foot."

"With a high-heeled shoe," said Olive, as she scurried up the stairs, "Go put that fool dog in the house, one of you kids."

Somehow between them they got Katie into the car, and she lay back, shuddering. She hurt, and moreover Olive was known as a fantastically dangerous driver, of the kind which never has an accident, although causing nervous breakdowns in drivers of other cars, pedestrians and passengers. She didn't have a car of her own, but on weekends she drove her husband's. He stayed home.

Elvira was waiting at the office. There were no steps to negotiate and shortly after she and Olive got Katie inside, Ben drove up.

"I'll wait and take her home," Olive pledged.

The reception room offered lots of lovely medical magazines, some of them hair-raising.

"Where's Jeremy?" asked Ben.

"God knows. Out somewhere with a redhead."

"Ha!" Ben commented, unbelievingly.

After the X ray, Ben told her, "No breaks, but a bad sprain. . . . Elvira, see if you can get Jeremy at the house."

She could and did; he'd just come in. She explained briefly, adding, "Ben's following in his car, to see that she's made comfortable."

"Famous last words," muttered Katie, who had decided she'd never walk again.

At Baker Street after everyone had departed—Olive, Ben and the boys who had rushed over to make the scene—Jeremy brought her something to eat on a tray, following a good stiff drink. "I called your mother," he said. "She'll be here tomorrow."

"Why? What for? The guest room isn't even made up!"

"I can make beds," said Jeremy. "She'll look after you, she'll cook—maybe a pot roast," he added wistfully.

"I haven't had time to ask but what exactly were you doing out with Beth Nelson? Walking through winter wonderland?"

"Actually, we were driving, in her car. Her mother has an old aunt who's about to go into a nursing home and she's getting rid of stuff. Beth remembered seeing some books in the attic and thought I should have a look at them. There's always a wild hope that you'll find a Tamerlane in the attic."

"What's that? A new type of monster?"

"A book. I'll explain later. As a matter of fact, I did find three comparatively valuable books."

"If you hadn't left that glaze of ice——" began Katie.

"I swept the steps," he said.

"But overlooked a little patch of snow," she said crossly.

"If so, I'm sorry, darling."

"And if you'd been at the shop and not gallivanting off looking for stupid books——"

"One of which I've had an order for, for three years."

Katie burst into tears, and Jeremy sat down and held her. He said, again, "I'm so sorry."

"Oh," she said sniffling. "It wasn't really your fault. I'd forgotten to put on the light. It's just that I hurt."

After a while he carried her upstairs, helped her undress and hop to the bathroom. "I'll get you a cane," he promised.

"Wheelchair," said Katie and smiled suddenly. She added, "I really don't deserve you," and then, thoughtfully, "Or maybe I have just what I deserved."

He got her to bed and said, "I'll make up your mother's room in the morning."

"Was she upset?"

"No. I think she was glad of an excuse to come down. There's something on our Susy's mind. But you'll have plenty of time to find out what."

"Mrs. Warner!" Katie exclaimed.

"What about her?"

"You call her, Jeremy. I haven't the strength."

Jeremy called Emily at her house and, when he hung up, Katie asked, "What did she say?"

"She's sorry, too. Says take it easy. Says you'd have saved money—providing we have insurance—if you'd gone to Emergency instead of to Ben."

"She would," said Katie.

"She was quite sympathetic for her. You have an addled attitude toward her. Emily likes you. She's a slave driver, of course, but she thinks you're quite a gal. She told me so the night of the C of C dinner."

"I didn't know she was there."

"Don't you read the local press? She ever favored us with a short speech—a very good one, too."

"What time does Mother expect to get here tomorrow?"

"About nine. I'll stay until she comes. I'll wash you, conduct you to the facilities, feed and dress you, and get you downstairs, after which, Susy, heaven bless her, will take over." He went into the bathroom and returned with a glass of water. "Here's your sleeping pill," he said. "Take it. You need sleep and so do I."

Susan Norton arrived at Baker Street shortly after nine the next morning driving a bright green VW. She walked in the front door, shouted, "Hi," and Jeremy came out to meet her. "Hello," he said, kissing her with enthusiasm. "Katie's in the living room looking rather like the Dying Gladiator, in drag. I'll get your luggage. I hope there's a lot. We expect you to stay for Christmas or even forever."

Susan Norton laughed. She was small, and waged an intermittent war with weight. Katie looked rather like her, but had her father's eyes.

"Don't forget to bring in the packages," she said. "Of course I'll stay until after the holidays."

She marched into the living room and said, "Well, Katie, you picked the right time. I was about to call and ask you could I come? Saves me postage on the presents."

She leaned down to kiss her daughter's cheek. "You look like an attractive ruin," she told her, "and I don't mean your ankle. You obviously don't eat. Well, that'll change now. Does Jeremy get home in time for me to go to the supermarket?"

Jeremy came in with luggage and Christmas packages. He said, "I'll take these upstairs. . . . Did I hear something about supermarket?"

"Of course. Last time I was here Katie phoned for groceries to the most expensive place in town. I shop. Anything on your special son-in-law diet?"

"Pot roast, boiled dinner, chicken fricassee with dumplings," Jeremy answered hungrily. "Not all at once. For tonight there are things in the freezing compartment you can whip up. I'll just feast my eyes on you."

"What shall I do with the car?"

"Leave it out front. I've put Katie's up. When I get home, I'll park your racing vehicle by the garage."

"Racing?"

"I've always thought you had a VW chassis on a Ferrari engine," said Jeremy, "the way you get around. See you before supper." He hugged her, and went over to kiss Katie. "You might know she'd fall over a dog," he said fondly.

"Ice," corrected Katie, glaring.

"Will you be all right while I unpack?" asked her mother.

"I'll be fine." Just looking at Susy made her feel fine. Somehow Katie, since her marriage, hadn't thought of Susy Norton as her mother, but as an excellent, sensible, and amusing friend.

"I won't be long, and I'll take any telephone calls in your bedroom. Here's your radio. I must have marked you. I listened to radio a lot, before you were born. I'll return presently and then I'll fix you an eggnog—provided you have eggs. If not I can borrow from Olive. Then you must tell me everything that's happened. Your infrequent letters are not exactly illuminating."

While her mother was trotting about upstairs—Susy was

not a noisy woman, but she did manage to make herself heard, walking, unpacking, whistling—Katie listened to the radio and wondered what was happening at the office. She had a meeting next week, Women's League of Voters—she'd have to skip it; and now that the Christmas-seal bit was over, there would be the Easter seal. She tried to keep up with community activities. Before her marriage she'd done small volunteer chores at the hospital. Now there simply wasn't time for everything—not if you worked and were married. How women with children managed committees and organizations she didn't know.

She heard the telephone and instinctively tried to get to her feet, but stopped in time. She also heard Susy's brisk voice in the so-called master bedroom. "I wonder what Women's Lib thinks of that?" she asked herself, and chuckled. Mistress wouldn't serve, or would it?

Susy's voice drifted through the open bedroom door and downstairs and Katie caught few phrases. "No, of course not. . . . Yes, she'll be all right. . . . But I told you I wouldn't be home until after the holidays. . . . Yes, I know, but we'll celebrate then. . . . No, I haven't told her. . . . Yes I'll be in touch. Keep an eye on things, will you?"

When the voice was stilled Katie thought: Mrs. Freeman? The Freemans were Susy's neighbors. Could be yes. Or Hank? He was the man who came to cut grass and who checked on the house when Susy was away, which wasn't often. He also forwarded the mail. No it couldn't be Hank.

Gnawed by curiosity, she contained herself until Susy, having changed to a short wool skirt and a pullover, came down again. "Who was that?" Katie began.

"For me," Susy replied firmly. "Hold your r.p.m.'s. Egg-nog coming up," she muttered, clattering into the kitchen from which in a moment she cried, "Eggs, thank heaven!"

She returned with the eggnog on a tray. "Dash of bourbon," she said. "Drink it all and slowly," and sat down in the big chair nearby. "You really looked wretched. Have you seen Ben Irvington?"

"Yes. Jeremy insisted. Waste of money. I'm just tired. Of course I saw him again when I sprained my fool ankle. . . . Who was that on the phone?"

"I told you it was for me. Roger Baines."

"Who on earth's that?"

"You and Jeremy met him briefly last time you came up, which now seems years ago. Remember, drinks at the Freemans'?"

"Well, just vaguely," Katie answered, trying.

"He's not spectacular," said her mother. "I told you at the time he'd moved just around the corner. Came from Boston, six or eight months before."

Katie said, "I do remember; pleasant, friendly, a widower you told me, and retired."

"That's right. He has a couple of children, both married, one in Arizona, one in California and a smattering of grandkids."

Katie said, round-eyed, "So you have a new boyfriend?"

"Well, in a manner of speaking. Now tell me about the Bankses, all the Irvingtons, the people I know, and those I don't—and drink that eggnog. I've looked around your establishment. We'll have soup for lunch, which I'll set up in here—and you'll have creamed chicken. Not that I approve of your using the ready-to-heat-and-serve products. Too expensive, but you do buy the best brands. For me, soup is all. I'm dieting again."

"Hold on," said Katie. "Are you serious about your new follower?"

"Roger? Well sometimes yes, and sometimes no."

"How could you cope with grown children and grandchildren, all the visiting and stuff?"

Susy said, "They're not mine. It's easier that way. Speaking of grandchildren, when are you and Jeremy———?"

Katie said hastily, "Not yet, not for a long time and I don't know why you raise your eyebrows. Frankly, I don't think you wanted to have me."

"Frankly, I didn't," her mother acknowledged. "I felt child bearing, when unplanned, was a sort of trap. Your father, however, was pleased. Incidentally, what made you think that?"

"Because I never believed after I was six or seven that you were the maternal type."

After a moment Susan Norton said slowly, "I'm sorry, Katie."

"I'm just trying to say that I'm not either," Katie told her.

After that, they talked Little Oxford, and Katie told her about Ross Cameron. She said, "We're going there Christmas if I have to crawl. He'll love having you. Jeremy says so and besides you must see that house."

"I have," Susy reminded her, "and I didn't blame Jeremy for refusing to buy it. But for a bachelor with an occasional child—I suppose that's what she'll be if the mother has custody—it should be perfection."

Later, with her sturdy mother's assistance, Katie went upstairs, and presently slept a little and Mrs. Norton sat in the attractive guest bedroom and thought: I've always known she felt cheated. And then, thinking of Roger Baines, she thought further: At my age? (which wasn't quite fifty) and at his? (which was sixty-four; he'd retired at sixty-two) and both of us set in our ways?

In the afternoon, before Jeremy came home, Katie and her mother had a companionable cup of tea and talked. Susy especially wanted to know about the Bankses.

"We were there Thanksgiving and haven't seen them since," said Katie.

"How are their children?"

"Angus and his beautiful Jamaican wife are off somewhere in Central America. He's an engineer. Remember? And she likes to teach; she's fluent in several languages. Roberta was there Thanksgiving with her nice husband and baby—they live in New York; Harriet's out west somewhere, in a commune. It's difficult for her father to accept that, and he was upset too about Angus' marriage. Jessica seems to accept things as they are."

"She's a rare woman," said Susy. "I wish I were like her; wish a lot of people were. Tell me about the Irvingtons."

Jeremy came in about six and Susy said, "But I haven't time to get to the market!"

"Tomorrow," said Jeremy firmly. "I'll come home early. Don't tell me you can't feed us!"

"Well, steak," said Susy, "and there are vegetables and salad makings. Tomorrow then. I'll shop around."

"We've charge accounts—" Katie began, but her mother said, "Forget them. I don't go just to one or two places. I'll stock up for the weekend or longer and Jeremy can pay me back."

Over drinks, Katie told her husband, "Mom's thinking of getting married, to a gent named Roger Baines. We met him at the Freemans."

"I remember him very well," Jeremy said. "I liked him . . . When's all this to be? May I give you away?"

"I was afraid of that," said Susy, "however I interpret the question. But hold on! I haven't made up my mind."

"Why not?"

"It's late for me, and later for him." She looked at her daughter. "Your father died suddenly," she reminded her. "I don't think I could go through that again."

Jeremy said, "It's a chance we all take."

"And I'd have to live a vicarious life," Susy said seriously, "I don't know that I can. I've always been independent."

"Why wouldn't you be if you remarried?"

"It would have to be his life. Oh, I don't mean his family. He wants to travel, and I'd like that. I never had the opportunity, but he's the sort of man who is used to making all the decisions and arrangements."

"Wouldn't you like that for a change?" asked Jeremy, smiling.

"Sometimes, I think so; sometimes, not."

"It's not much of a price to pay, provided you're fond of him and compatible otherwise," Jeremy argued. "Everyone, I suppose, at any age pays a price for love, companionship and security—and I don't mean financial security. It's a question of need, I guess. I'm sure he needs you, Susy, and, if you discover that you need him too, then you'll pay the price willingly."

Susy said after a moment, "Actually, that's what I came here to find out."

11

✳✳✳✳ Katie woke before dawn next morning. Her ankle hurt, but the swelling was down somewhat. She was groggy from the sleeping pill, and her head ached. It was dark and a fitful north wind rattled somewhere at the windows.

"Can't sleep?" asked Jeremy, yawning. "It's still very early. . . . Hurting much?"

"I keep waking up. Yes, I hurt," Katie said.

"How about a pain pill?"

"I'm sick of medication and it's no cure."

"Of course not; just for pain and inability to sleep. Try to, for a little while."

He was half whispering, in order not to wake their guest and Katie said crossly, "You needn't mutter. Mom sleeps like a log."

"Silly expression, if ever I heard one."

He switched on the light and Katie blinked. "What's that for?" she demanded.

"I'll try to make you more comfortable." He got out of bed, adjusted her pillows and the covers, and said, "Poor little ankle."

"Damned little ankle!"

"Whatever you say. . . . Want me to take you to the bathroom?"

"No, thanks."

"Well, as long as I'm up . . ." he said, and vanished. On his return he leaned down to kiss her. "Try to doze, Katie," he said.

He got into bed, turned off the light, patted her round shoulder. "You've been pretty good about this," he told her, "not heroic, but good."

He was almost asleep when she asked, "Do you think Mom will marry Roger Baines?"

"I don't know. Are you going to advise her?"

"No. You did, though."

"Just in a philosophical way. It's not up to either of us to make a big thing of it."

"But it's her life!"

"That's what I implied; it isn't ours."

She was silent, looking into darkness and he'd drifted off again when she spoke. "About her needing this Roger person . . ."

He said patiently through his drowsy fog, "What about it? I think she does need him. It's a lonely business for her, Katie, and she has probably a quarter of a century ahead of her."

Katie said, "But she never seemed to need anyone that I could determine—not me, not even my father."

"She's older now, darling; that's the reason."

"But how can she adjust? She's never had to. Everyone has always adjusted to her, in a way."

"Maybe she'll learn; we all have to, however young or old. If she needs him, it won't be too difficult."

"Do we need each other, Jeremy?"

"Katie, for heaven's sake!"

"What for?" she demanded. "Aside from sleeping, eating, and being together weekends, Sundays, holidays, evenings. . . ?"

"Same reasons I gave Susy: love, companionship and security."

"Before we were married I thought a lot about companionship. I felt sorry for Linda. I figured that's one thing she'd never have; she and Tom were always fighting. They still do."

"Not very seriously, Katie. Just a release of tensions, I assume. Also, they're really fighting on the same side, which makes them comrades."

"Everything you say," she complained, "is too pat, as if you were explaining a psychology primer to a child."

She heard him laugh. "Perhaps I am," he agreed.

"What's companionship really? The same work, you selling in the bookshop or me selling houses. The same preferences in music, athletics, food, movies, people?"

"It's very simple, being needed is basically love."

"I love you," said Katie and touched his cheek, "but I don't think I need you. Well . . . not all the time and I'm sure you don't need me all the time."

"I come from a family of needers," Jeremy told her. "My parents needed each other and me; I needed them. Which is not to say we were together twenty-four hours a day or saw eye to eye about everything."

"We should never have married," said Katie, growing sleepy. "I told you we should just have lived together when we wanted to——"

"Ah!" said her husband. "Open marriage? It has its drawbacks however, like any other kind."

But now she was asleep.

"Be thankful," Jeremy told himself, "for small mercies." But he was very troubled. He had realized since he first met and loved her that Katie Norton was her own man, so to speak. Flying her independence like a banner. This, he had also loved, being himself a whole person. He'd also known she was ambitious. He was not, in the money or prestige-seeking sense. He worked hard, he wished, reasonably, to earn sufficient for his and—after marriage—her needs and to accumulate enough for emergencies. He wanted to be a seller of books, and a not-too-cautious buyer. He had believed that, in a marriage, adjustment is never total but that it builds over the years. He still believed that. But from the middle of this second year, he had observed Katie's increasing restlessness and the friction, while not, he thought, of any great consequence, also troubled him. One of his reasons for wanting a child was that he thought they needed a shared responsibility. They'd discussed having children before they were married and she'd said firmly, "Give me a few years—four, even five. I don't want to be tied down in nine months, or a year."

He'd argued that he hadn't meant so soon. "And you could still work after a while," he assured her. "We'll build a house; we'll have proper help to take care of a baby."

But she was adamant.

Katie was more like her mother than he'd realized. She had told him about Susan, drawing her own conclusions. Susan hadn't planned for a child. "Guesswork on my part," Katie had said, "but it always seemed to me that she resented me, in a way, Not that I hampered her. After I was six or so, I could take care of myself."

She could; she was herself.

God knows, he thought, watching the gray dawn filter through the windows, listening to the cold wind sigh, subside and rise again. I've never wanted her to live through—and for—me.

He turned over and told himself, "No. That's not an honest statement. Certainly almost every man hopes for such a relationship with his wife. Few achieve it, so most adjust and compromise.

Family was important to him; he'd enjoyed the security of being part of a family, and regretted that he was an only child, as Katie was. The parents of an only child were in jeopardy. Give a man and woman four, five, or six, children and there was probability of a continuance, a non-theological immortality.

Snow fell, and Little Oxford glistened when the sun shone. Everyone was busy. Jeremy at the bookshop was swamped with women rushing in and crying, "I can't think of anything for Bert's Aunt Regina. Do you have a nice romantic *decent* book or maybe an illustrated one on London? She adores London."

Katie limped painfully about. "A sprain can sometimes be worse than a break," Ben told her.

And she said, "I've a very low threshold of pain and I hate being handicapped."

Jeremy brought her a cane, cut to fit her height and Susy, poking about various shops, came upon a pair of elegant laced boots.

"For heaven's sake," cried Katie as they were proudly exhibited to her, "where did you get these?"

"Have you ever been in a shop called, rather unfortunately, 'Past Time'? Two words."

"On Willow Street? I've seen it. The kids go there. There's a demand for people's old clothes, specially of the twenties, I believe. I've never been inside."

"These shoes go back further." Susy turned one in her hand. "Apparently never worn," she added, admiring the bronze kid. "There was a pair in your grandmother's attic. More pointed a toe as I remember it. Also some high buttoned shoes. Actually, they had a pair of those at Past Time . . . with black heels and toes and tan suede uppers, but they were too small for you and I doubt that you have a buttonhook. Try this on your good foot. They do give considerable support, or so the nice young man assured me. It was a few minutes before I realized he was a man. I can bring them back, he said, if you don't want them. He gave me a receipt. Seems they're all the rage as we're undergoing a fit of nostalgia."

Katie tried on the boot and her mother said, "I'll lace it. . . . There, how's that?"

"Fine, I guess."

"Try the other one."

"I still hurt, Mom."

"But there's no swelling. If you can't bear it, I'll take the pair back."

Katie gingerly inserted her foot into the boot, yelped, but persevered. Her mother laced it for her.

"Now, try to walk," she said. "Use the cane if you're scared."

Katie took one uncertain step, then another. She said reluctantly, "You're right. I can walk."

"Okay, so we'll keep them and you can go into the new year fashionably, even if you're limping a little."

"How much did they cost?"

"A fortune. Be my guest," said Susy grandly.

Katie was limping around when Jeremy came home. He cast his overcoat and hat into a corner and said, "I don't believe it!"

"Mom found them at the creepy little Past Time place."

"It may be creepy, but the owners are cleaning up. . . . I'll have to look through costume books to pin your shoes down as to date, but they're most becoming."

"Anything for a laugh," Katie said gloomily.

"Nonsense! You're high fashion. And you can walk."

People came to see her before Christmas. The Bankses one evening after supper and before they left Susy made coffee and little sandwiches. "To celebrate Katie's footwear," she explained, "a collation!"

They had conversation and music and Jeremy and Gordon Banks smoked their pipes in amity. Jessica, speaking to Susan, said softly, "You've a decision to make, haven't you?"

"Haven't we all?" inquired Susy cautiously.

"I'm not trying to pry. You'll make it, if not here, then after you return home."

"Yes or no?" asked Susy against her will.

"It would be good if it's yes," said Jessica, "but it's your decision, not mine."

Later, cleaning up, Susy remarked, "Jessica Banks scares me."

Jeremy, leaning against the refrigerator, asked, "Why? As if I didn't know."

"She reads minds."

"I don't think so. Jessica's sensitive to other people. Call it ESP or whatever you wish. Her family's used to it; so are her friends."

"Disconcerting anyway and I've no intention of letting her influence me."

"Of course not," Jeremy agreed.

Mrs. Latimer dropped by with a small covered basket filled with freshly made scones and a couple of jars of home-made preserves. She consented to a cup of tea, and she and Susy got along famously.

Cam came one evening for Susy's boiled dinner. He told her she was not only a magnificent cook—"Don't tell Polly Latimer I said that"—but prettier than Katie. Susy was drawn to him immediately as was inevitable.

Jeremy brought in their tree, not very tall but fat and full branched and he and Susy trimmed it with advice from the sidelines. "Too symmetrical," Katie complained, "too regimented. Mix things up, 'specially the colors. Here." She limped over and made an adjustment. "Like that," she said. "Christmas trees shouldn't look trimmed—just gay and bright and glowing. Please no tinsel. I hate things that drip." She looked at her mother. "Our trees were lovely," she said, remembering.

"Your father's work," Susy said. "The popcorn balls and the strings of popcorn and cranberries. I made 'em, but he trimmed. And we had the red apples and the wooden angels, which were in his family for ages. They're in the attic now —the angels."

"May I have them sometime?"

"Why, of course. I haven't had a regular tree for years— just little table ones."

When Christmas came, they exchanged their gifts after a stupendous breakfast, and to the sound of carols. It was a dazzlingly bright day and the light snow was soft as lace on the trees. The roads had been cleared and Katie said, "About Cam's party. You still think I should wear these ridiculous shoes?"

"He liked them," Jeremy reminded her. "So did Gordon and Jessica. Mrs. Latimer fairly wept over them. Of course."

"I'll look so foolish in a long dress."

"Wear your new one. That's what I bought it for!"

It was bronze, paler than the high laced shoes, with golden lights; short, high necked, long sleeved and the skirt very full. He'd given her other things. The perfume she liked and a little fur muff.

Susy gave her practical gifts. "My chief one being the shoes," she informed her.

For Susy there were things which Katie had selected before her accident and Jeremy brought her a book on ecology. For Jeremy, Susy had ties and tobacco and Katie gave him a gold key, uncut.

"It's for our house when we get it," she explained.

"Is that a hint?"

"Broader than a barn," Katie said. "Come spring, let's find an empty acre or so, or a house we can remodel."

"Merry Christmas," said Jeremy.

12

✳✳✳✳ A little after the appointed hour, the Jeremy Palmers and Susan Norton arrived at the Cameron house. Jeremy drove up, extracted Katie and his mother-in-law from the car, and put Katie's cane in her hand. "Booted and spurred," he said, "to make a dramatic entrance."

" 'Lean on me,' " quoted Susy, " 'I'm 'most seven.' "

"You," said her daughter, "are nuts and I want to go home."

"You've never been exposed to Little Lord Fauntleroy," said Susy, "and it's too late to go home."

The door opened wide and Cam came out with Ronnie. "Come in. . . . Here, hang on me, Katie," and Ronnie, jumping up and down, cried, "What fantastic boots!"

"You've seen them before," said Katie. "Do find me a quiet corner, Cam."

And Susy said, "Preferably in the attic. . . . What a delightful house!"

"How about the study?" Cam asked. "Or would you rather not walk that far, Katie?"

"Any place," Katie told him. "Heavens, what a lot of people."

"Like wow," Ronnie suggested.

In the living room, Cam's guests were milling about, laughing, drinking, and making their way to the buffet.

"The bar's in the study," said Cam. "Gives them exercise to and fro. Here—a love seat and a table at your elbow. Ronnie, find out what Mrs. Palmer would like in the way of nourishment. I'll attend to the drinks. How about you, Mrs. Norton?"

Susy said, "I'll manage. I love buffets," and then, "There's Beth Nelson." She'd been in the bookshop, she knew Beth.

Katie's eyes widened. "How did you pull that off?" she asked her host.

"I just invited her," he said. "I'll be back in a moment, Katie; meantime, here's your husband."

Jeremy made his way toward her, stopping to talk as he advanced. Ronnie had vanished, after memorizing Katie's order. It was simple, "Just anything, dear," Katie had told her.

"Did you see Beth Nelson?" she asked Jeremy. Of course he had. She'd seen him stop beside her.

"Yes, and Emily Warner."

"She's here?"

"Stationed at the buffet."

Cam came with Katie's drink, a very dry martini. "Ronnie has your order? Where's your mother?" he asked.

"Sunk without trace, after saying something about finding her way to the study," Katie answered.

"It won't be difficult. The path is strewn with bodies."

He went off as Ronnie returned. "Hot chafing dish lobster," she said, offering a large tray. There was also cold chicken, a salad and rolls. "I'll come for your dessert order later. Four kinds, including mince pie. Yummy!"

Jeremy said, "I could eat a horse and I've no doubt Cam's supplied one. . . . The booze?"

"In the study. Mother's in there. Wait a minute. Who was that small dark woman you stopped to speak to?"

"Mrs. Niles. Haven't you ever seen her before?"

"Yes. Not close up. I'd love to meet her."

"So you shall. I'll be back unless unavoidably detained at the bar. Save me that minuscule space beside you."

He didn't come back for a while and Cam appeared with a tall blond gentleman in tow. He said, "Katie, this is one of my associates in nefarious business, Hal Evans. Hal, this is the beautiful, temporarily disabled wife of Jeremy Palmer whom you have met. Sit down beside her, but don't frighten her away."

He added, "Practically no one at this clambake sits—they stand around talking, gesturing, spilling, but, I hope, having fun. Look out for him, Katie. He's momentarily unattached."

Mr. Evans was attractive, attentive and pleasant and perhaps, she thought, hungry. "Have you had anything to eat?" she asked.

"Yes. I came early. I'm staying overnight in the study, but the way things look it will be morning before I retire. May I bring you a refill?"

"No, thanks," Katie said, adding, as Jeremy returned with his glass, "I believe you two know each other?"

"We've met several times at the University Club," said Jeremy, smiling. "Hi, Hal. What do you think of Cam's house?"

"Marvelous," Evans answered. "At least when it was almost empty and I had a chance to look round. Wish I could move to the country."

"Don't even think it. Handicapped as she is, my wife still

deals in real estate. Would you settle for a good book?"
Jeremy asked.

"Matter of fact," said Evans, "I met a remarkable woman
half an hour or so ago; she's in real estate; she cornered me
immediately in a nice, casual way. I explained that too much
alimony doesn't permit commuting."

"That's my boss," said Katie.

"Who's that very pretty redhead?" Evans asked and
Jeremy said promptly, "I'm *her* boss."

It was much later—after several people had come to talk
to Katie and then drift away and Ronnie had brought an
elegant trifle and coffee—when Jeremy, who had been cir-
culating "like a library," he informed his wife, returned with
Rosie Niles. Rosie, very thin, with a mop of curly black hair
and enormous dark eyes said, "I've been wanting to meet
you. Jessica has told me a good deal about you. I haven't
been here much, but now I'm back. Jessica has found another young singer for me; a boy this time, just out of college, working his head off as a salesman. He wanted to be a
teacher, but jobs are scarce."

"Please," said Katie, "won't you sit with me for a while?
May Jeremy freshen your drink?"

Rosie sat down and put the glass she was carrying on the
table beside her. "It's a tomato juice straight," she said, "and
I've had enough. I don't like tomato juice, or fruit juice or
soft drinks." Her big eyes sparkled, and she added, "I'm an
alcoholic, Katie—that's your name, isn't it?"

Jeremy said, "Call it ex, Mrs. Niles."

"There's no such thing as ex. Run away," she added, flip-
ping a small rather ugly hand, "and let me talk to your
wife."

Susy reappeared and Katie offered her the big footstool
which Cam had thoughtfully provided. And a little later, as
the people thinned out, Jeremy came to ask, "Had enough?"

Katie nodded. She had talked to a dozen strangers and those whom she knew, including Emily, who had marched up, asking, "How long before you can drive? . . . Actually you look extremely well. I think you're goldbricking."

Farewells were exchanged and Rosie said, "If you can't come to see me, I'll come to see you, Katie," and Evans, as Jeremy took his wife to the door, looked up from an earnest conversation with Beth Nelson to say, smiling, "I must get myself asked here often. Susy's very congenial people."

And Susy said, disconsolately, "I don't know why you want to go, children; it's such fun," and Ronnie came tearing up from somewhere, crying, "Mrs. Latimer sends regards and hopes you like the trifle. It's a specialty of the house."

Cam detached himself from a group, came to the door with them and waited while Jeremy got the car, Ronnie beside him. "You'll catch cold," said Katie, to the little girl, who sneezed twice, and said, "I never catch cold; it's so vulgar." But she squeezed Katie's hand and went back into the house.

"Shouldn't she be in bed?" asked Susy.

"Of course. Mrs. Latimer will arrive briskly, presently and shoo her off to slumber. . . . Did you have a good time, Katie?"

"I certainly did."

"How could I ever have cooked a dinner for you? I wouldn't dare after this," Susy said.

"You'd better or I'll close out my account with the bookshop," Cam warned her.

Jeremy drove up. Cam helped Susy and Katie in, and stood in the still star-spangled night, smiling. There was a waxing moon and the snow and trees were coated with silver.

On the way home Katie said, "There's something about Mrs. Niles . . . and I don't mean her appearance."

"Intensity," Jeremy said promptly. "She smolders with it."

"Surely she wasn't serious when she said she was an alcoholic?"

"I think she was, but I've never heard it discussed."

Susy said, "I liked her."

"I don't know much about her," Jeremy admitted, "except that she was born here, married a band leader at an early age, and was later widowed. She had earned quite a reputation as a blues singer in night clubs. Eventually she came back to Little Oxford."

"I've seen her house at a distance," Katie said. "She must be loaded."

"That's the general impression. Jessica is very fond of her. So are the Irvingtons, both sets. Rosie's main interest seems to lie in finding talented young singers and underwriting their training."

"If I had her money," Katie said dreamily, "I'd travel all over the world, and just have a little pad somewhere, between flights." She yawned. "I'm sleepy," she told them unnecessarily. "Were you there when Mrs. Warner said I was goldbricking?"

"No. . . . Tired of it?"

"I'm not goldbricking!"

"Have Ben check you over. Your ankle's bound to give you trouble for some time and driving in winter is a more than challenging chore."

"I'll go ape," said Katie.

"There's no reason why you can't go back to the office," Jeremy told her. "I'll drive you there and back."

"I'd be stuck with everyone else's paper work."

Susy said, "Six of one, half a dozen of the other. Either you'll crash your car or get claustrophobia. Suppose you give yourself until after the New Year? And thanks for taking me to the party, I loved it."

When they'd gone to bed, Jeremy asked, "So if you were rich you'd travel. How about me?"

"If I were rich," said Katie promptly, "I wouldn't be married to you. I'd never have met you if I was running around England, France, Greece, Italy, also Australia and the Far East. You wouldn't be picking me up at some bar in Switzerland, would you? Besides, even if I had met you, I'm sure you wouldn't have been interested in a rich, gorgeous brilliant woman."

"I couldn't stand her." He drew her closer. "Poor wretch, as unhappy as the little match girl."

"I'm not unhappy," Katie argued. "I love you. I love this town and my job. I even like this crazy house—which reminds me, the minute it's spring, promise we can look for a house or a place where we can build?" She didn't wait for the answer, "I've friends," she said. "I love a few, like most."

"What do you hate?"

"Cooking. Snails. A head cold, a sprained ankle and occasional cabin fever. . . . Do go to sleep, Jeremy."

But she didn't let him. She said, "Beth Nelson had herself quite a time tonight; all that attention. Especially Cam and Hal Evans. Is she usually so animated?"

"Well—yes—over books. She's young, Katie, and she's had a rough time. As for tonight, I'm glad she enjoyed it, but it worries me."

"Why? She's grown up."

"I know Cam too well."

"That's none of your business. You aren't responsible just because she works for you."

"With me," he corrected. "And I do feel responsible. I wish she could meet someone of a suitable age and remarry."

"Cam's not suitable?" Katie asked.

"No. And you've heard him sound off on the subject of marriage. I just don't want to see Beth involved."

"You stay out of it," ordered Katie.

They spent New Year's Eve at home, and New Year's Day at the Bankses. Cam had asked them for both occasions, but Jeremy had refused. "Without consulting me," said Katie indignantly.

"Did you really want to go?"

"No, but Mom would have liked it."

"Don't hide behind me," Susy told her. "One such party is all I can digest."

At the Bankses: "You've made up your mind, haven't you?" Jessica asked Susy.

"Just about," Susy admitted, thinking: What a lovely, gentle woman! Good clear through to her considerable backbone.

Jessica touched her guest's hand. "I'm glad," she said. "I know you'll be very happy."

"But I didn't tell you which way I'd made it up, or even what about," said Susy.

"It will work out," Jessica said seriously. . . . "Look at Katie. She looks rested and she's not nearly as nervous as she was."

Katie was talking to Rosie Niles, and Susy said, "Mrs. Niles came to see us after the Christmas shindig. She and Katie seem to have found something in common."

"They're both restless," Jessica said, "and both fighters."

The day Susy went home, it was snowing and Katie tried to make her stay.

"I've driven in blizzards," Susy reminded her. "Stop nagging."

Roger Baines had telephoned almost every day, and the evening before she left, Susy had announced, "I've decided to marry Roger, misgivings and all. Mine, I mean. I expect you two to come up and hold my hand. I'll let you know when. If the weather's bad, take the train. Jeremy can get away for one weekend." She paused, then said, "I do hope you'll like him."

"Would it make a difference if one or both of us didn't?"

"No, but I'd like filial approval."

Katie went back to the office the next day, and that night Tom Davis telephoned in the middle of the night.

"Jeremy? . . . This is Tom."

"What's wrong?"

"Linda, she's in the hospital. We were in an accident; She's lost the baby. She's very sick, Jeremy. Her folks are here but . . . will you and Katie come?"

"We'll be there," said Jeremy, "as soon as we can."

13

✻✻✻✻ Halfway to the hospital Katie broke a long silence. "Do you think they'll let us see her?" she asked.

"No. But we may be able to see Tom. Perhaps he told them at the reception desk that he phoned us. I don't know. He sounded completely distraught."

"Do you think she'll die?"

"Pull yourself together," Jeremy advised her, "or you'll be of no help to Tom. I haven't the remotest idea how serious it is, Katie."

"I wonder if she was driving?"

"What makes you say that?"

"They've a sort of rule—if they've been out, and Tom's had anything to drink, Linda drives."

Jeremy parked and they went up the steps, Katie holding his hand. At the main desk he explained that he knew how late it was, but that Mr. Davis had sent for them. The woman on duty knew him. She said, "Yes, Mr. Palmer. Mr. Davis is in the waiting room on the third floor. Mrs. Davis' brother and his wife just left. . . . Oh, Doctor Irvington."

Ben came up and leaned over the desk. "What's up?" he asked Katie.

"An accident . . . Linda Davis—you remember her? We lived together in Little Oxford?"

"Of course. I remember when she had pneumonia. Let me know if I can help. Have to run now. I'm waiting for Pop to show up to see Old Mrs. Foster," and he loped off.

A moment later Katie and Jeremy were in the elevator and then on the third floor. Everything was quiet, but now and then there were sounds—a bell ringing, intercom, calls for doctors, someone crying.

"I hate it," said Katie under her breath.

Tom was alone in the waiting room; the ashtray beside him was piled high. He had a bandage across his temple, and his arm was in a sling.

"Am I glad to see you!"

"How is she?" Jeremy asked.

"Pretty sick. She's in intensive care. My God," he added, "it was terrible! Cops, ambulances, Linda screaming, glass all over the road."

"What happened, exactly?"

"How in hell do I know? Just a car barrelling out of nowhere. I was driving; Linda grabbed the wheel—that's it. She—she has internal injuries," he said.

"And you?" asked Jeremy, sitting beside him on the small couch.

"Bash on the head, no concussion; chipped bone in my wrist."

"They said at the desk that your brother-in-law had gone home."

"Fred? Yes, with Doris. . . . We're going to need a lawyer," said Tom, "as well as doctors and maybe surgeons. That guy was driving like a lunatic." He stubbed out his cigarette and added dully, "I blame myself. Linda will blame herself and I suppose we'll both blame each other. She was so scared, she didn't know what she was doing, poor kid." He blinked back the difficult tears. "She had to be told she'd lost her baby. She was conscious when she got here."

Jeremy said, "Let us take you home. You can't do anything here."

"They just let me look at her for a minute," said Tom forlornly. "There are six patients in there. Once she's in a room of her own, they'll try to get specials."

"There's no use staying the rest of the night," Jeremy said. "You'll be called if it's necessary and you can come back early."

Katie said stoutly, "We'll stay with you, Tom."

They left a short time later after Tom had talked to the doctor on emergency, who had admitted them, and to their own doctor from their town, who had been called to the hospital and was still there. He spoke to Jeremy also. He said, "I told Tom he could go home. Glad you're here." He shook his head. He'd known Linda since she was a child. "It's a bad business. But she's young and healthy, and tomorrow—that is, today—we'll have consultants. . . . There's no use looking in, Tom," he added. "She's under sedation."

He opened the bag he carried, shook some capsules into an envelope and handed them to Jeremy. "See that he gets two of these," he ordered, "so he can sleep. I'll dress the head injury again tomorrow. It's not serious. Neither is the chipped bone, but they're painful and he's had a bad shock."

The Palmers took Tom home in the still cold night. Once he said, "The guy could have skidded, going so fast; there's ice."

Jeremy asked, "Was he injured?"

"I guess so; he was bleeding. The police talked to him. They were still there when the ambulance came."

Two or three times he asked of no one in particular, "Why did it have to happen?"

Katie said, herself not convinced, "Tom, she's going to be all right."

"We were always fighting," Tom said, as if to himself. "Ever since we were kids. I was older of course, and she bugged me, tagging around after me. But it was fun later and exciting and we always made up. She said awhile back, 'After the baby's old enough to understand, and even before, if we have arguments, he mustn't hear them.' She was sure it was a boy. 'Kids whose parents yell at each other grow up insecure,' she said. . . . She wanted that baby so much. Me too——"

"There'll be others," Jeremy predicted.

"How do you know? The damned doctors won't say anything."

He was silent a moment, then: "I'd better call Fred, he can get me back to the hospital."

"We'll call him."

At the Davis house, Tom said, "I could use a drink—I wasn't drunk, you know, when it happened. I had one belt at the Powells' before dinner. Linda had some wine."

"You're going to take these capsules, Tom," Jeremy reminded him, "and alcohol isn't indicated."

Katie stayed downstairs while Jeremy took Tom up and helped him undress. Looking at the neat figure-eight bandage on his wrist, Tom said, "It would have been better if it had been me instead of Linda."

Katie called Linda's brother. She said, "We'll stay the rest of the night. Could you or Doris manage to come after breakfast?"

Later she tiptoed upstairs. Tom was drowsily incoherent and Jeremy sitting beside him said quietly, "He'll soon drop off. Go lie down in the guest room, darling, and try to get some sleep."

"Fred will be here right after breakfast," she reported. She looked around and felt her throat close and her eyes sting. This room was ninety-nine percent Linda. She was a spotless but not tidy housekeeper and she and Katie had lived happily in their small apartment in a welter of each other's belongings. Here, Linda's clothes were draped over a chair, shoes had been kicked off, there was spilled face powder on the glass top of the dressing table and the perfume she affected was still apparent. There was very little evidence of Tom, other than his masculine highboy. It was a pretty, frilly cluttered bedroom and very Linda.

The guest room by contrast was neat and impersonal.

Katie was lying, clothed to her boots, across one of the beds when Jeremy came in. "Not asleep?" he asked.

"I can't . . . I keep thinking."

He left the door open and lay down beside her on the narrow bed. He said, "I'll hear him if he even moves. Here" —he put his arm around her—"close your eyes. When I get you home, you can go to bed for the rest of the day."

"Mrs. Warner will have a convulsion."

"Let her."

"How about the shop?"

"I'll call Mary Hawes at her house. She'll take over. Be quiet, baby."

"It's so pitiful," she said. "Poor Linda—poor Tom. . . . I don't pray often, Jeremy, except when I'm wildly happy or something wonderful happens. Then I say thank you in my heart. But I've been lying here, trying to. It's strange, but this is something I've never experienced before. Oh, I've known of accidents, deaths—but no one close to me was ever badly hurt. My father's death was my only real loss. It isn't that I don't like people; I do, but I guess I've never been deeply involved with anyone but my father and you. I'm fond of a lot of people. I love very few. Linda's one. I never thought much about it until tonight."

He listened quietly as she went on, "I think that's one reason why I haven't wanted a child. I'd have to be involved. I'd be responsible for its being here. My mother wasn't much involved with me, beyond seeing that I was healthy, had a suitable education, proper recreation and playmates. She supervised my diet and watched over my posture, my skin and hair—that one hundred strokes a night. . . . She taught me simple biology when I was quite small. When I was older, she graded the boys I dated. Excellent to good, passing or failures. She was like a kind, busy, older sister with authority —you could call it clout, I guess. We've been closer, really, since I came to Little Oxford, and especially since we were married, Jeremy."

He said, "You've missed a good deal, Katie," and thought: If we have a child will she remember that and make it up to her—or him?

He felt her tighten in his arms, almost as if, like Jessica, he had reached her mentally. But all she said was, "I'm scared. Things happen so fast, things that change your life."

"I honestly believe that Linda will be all right, dear," he told her.

She began to cry then, against his shoulder, and he said, stroking her hair, "That's right, let go."

After a while she slept, a little and lightly; Jeremy not at all. And when he heard Tom stirring, he rose. He said, "Katie, I'm going to go in to Tom. There's a bathroom between this and the other guest room. You can freshen up a little, then how about breakfast?"

All she said was, "I hate waking up. . . . All right, Jeremy," and added, "I left my lipstick and compact downstairs in my handbag."

"I'll bring it up in a moment," he promised from the doorway and Katie sat up, looked at him and asked, "Did you know Linda was going to turn this room into a nursery?"

"No, but it figures."

"Blue," said Katie, "for a boy."

She thought, going into the bathroom, how she'd laughed and asked: "Suppose it's a girl?" and Linda had answered, "But it won't be."

"It's a fifty-fifty chance," Katie had remarked, "unless there are more accurate statistics."

"Well, if it's a girl, I won't send her back and blue's pretty. I can inject a dash of pink here and there, but Tom wants a son. Most men do," Linda said.

Jeremy came in with the handbag and Katie said, "Kiss me good morning."

Jeremy did so and Katie murmured, "Thanks, love, that helps."

As everyone except Katie had predicted, Linda recovered. Katie and Jeremy saw her several times in the hospital after she was out of the intensive care unit. And later, at home, after several early suppers. Katie wasn't driving yet. Her ankle still plagued her and, to her intense and out-spoken annoyance, Jeremy was afraid of the roads for her.

"I can manage. I'm not crippled and I'm a cautious driver!"

"Be patient," said Jeremy.

Twice he suggested that Beth Nelson take her to the Davises' house. "She's doing a little scouting job for me in Deeport," he explained. "She can drop you off at Linda's and pick you up in an hour or so."

It was impossible not to like Beth, Katie thought, her honesty tempered by envy. In the first place, she was beau-tiful and intelligent, and, thought Katie, very fortunate for she was around Jeremy more than was Katie. She was gentle, kind, and possessed a pixie humor.

"How you can see that girl day in and out," Katie told him one night, "and not fall madly in love with her, I can't imagine."

"I don't do anything madly," said Jeremy. "I'm a logical guy. Rather like Mr. Spock."

Sometimes they watched the reruns of *Star Trek* together.

"You're not as attractive," said Katie critically, "I adore his ears and eyebrows. But to return to your exposure to Beth Nelson. . . ."

"It's fine," said Jeremy, "as I'm not ready to fall in love again. Probably not ever," he added thoughtfully. "I realize Beth is handsomer than you and smarter. It's the latter quality which scares me."

"It doesn't scare Cam. She told me she's been seeing him when he's here."

"She's *too* smart," said Jeremy, "to be disturbed by Cam. It will take a very solid character to interest Beth—clever, intelligent as well as intellectual. There's a difference. A man of principle, older than herself, a good guy, somewhat square, wholly reliable and emotionally stable."

"Like yourself?" Katie inquired.

"Like me," Jeremy agreed gravely. "Did I also mention charming? Not Cam's sort of charm, of course. The trouble is, I'm in love with my wife and Beth isn't in love with me. So don't lose any sleep—at least not over Mrs. Nelson."

Katie laughed. She said, "You're impossible."

"Elementary," responded Jeremy. "Tell me about Linda."

Linda was progressing. She had told Katie, "It will take a while. Seems that my baby assembly line is all shook up, not that I can't have a baby, but not for a while. Doctor's orders—three of them."

"Babies?"

"Doctors. So I'll be patient. But Tom's frightened. He keeps saying we don't need a child, which is absurd. Of course we do. But there's time. And this guilt business—his and mine—has faded, sort of, like a photograph. We've promised never to blame ourselves or each other again."

Linda was out of bed for a lengthening period of time each day and they'd found a good sensible woman to do the cleaning and cooking except breakfast, which Tom organized and took upstairs to Linda. "He's only dropped the tray twice," Linda said. "Poor lamb! Ella costs an arm and a leg, but she's worth it. The hospital cost both arms and legs, but that was worth it, too. We'll manage. Tom has good hospitalization insurance."

Early in February, Susan Norton was married to Roger Baines. There was a break in the weather and the Palmers drove up on a Saturday morning, started home after the reception, spent the night at a motel and reached home Sunday. It had been a big wedding, as Susan knew almost everyone in town and people whom she didn't know sneaked into back pews. A big reception also, at Susan's. Her house was on the market and Susy said hopefully to Katie, "Maybe we have prospective buyers. The house looks so lovely. I'll miss it very much."

They'd live in Roger's house when they weren't traveling.

Roger's children and grandchildren were present; his son was best man and Katie was Susy's only attendant. They had a private talk before the ceremony. "I so hope you'll be happy," Katie told her.

"I've always been—if not happy, then contented. Except of course when your father died. Roger and I are good friends and most compatible. Also, we love each other.

There will be adjustments, but we're not too set in our ways to make them."

Katie and Jeremy liked Roger, a quiet forthright man with warmth and humor, but that night at the motel, Katie said, "It's so hard to imagine."

"What is?"

"My mother——"

"As a bride? But Susy's a young woman, Katie. Surely you don't find her remarriage distasteful?"

"Maybe," said Katie reluctantly.

"Love," said Jeremy, "is not the sole prerogative of the young, nor is sex, and the need to belong, to be close."

"I suppose so," Katie admitted. She looked around the pleasant impersonal room. A north wind tapped on the windowpanes. She said, "There's something so delightfully sinful about being in a motel with your husband. I felt that way on the Cape—remember when you and I were there for a week while the shop was being repainted?"

"I remember."

"Can't we go back sometime?"

"We can," Jeremy promised, "when I can get away . . . . Katie, if it isn't snowing here tomorrow, how would you like to help with the driving?"

"I'd like to," said Katie, her head against his shoulder and Jeremy said, "Let's turn off that damned TV; we're not watching it anyway."

And Katie said sleepily, "I wonder how mother will like Hawaii. I'd love to go to Hawaii."

"You shall," said Jeremy, "when I'm as old and rich as your stepfather."

So at last she was driving again. And Mrs. Warner, equipped with new garments, some of them outrageous, had gone off on her cruise, and Katie was very busy at the office.

Business hadn't picked up much, but it would. You could see the days lengthening now in February. March could be devastating or pleasantly splendid; April could be anything. Everyone and his rich—or poor—uncle would be buying or selling houses.

14

✳✳✳✳ The blizzard crept into Little Oxford overnight like a whisper rather than a scream. None of the weathermen had predicted it. "Light snow," they cheerfully informed readers, watchers, and listeners. But around the Little Oxford area old timers squinted at the sky, announced something was in the making, filled oil lamps, checked oil heaters and used bathtubs and every big receptacle in their houses for water, if they had wells, as many did.

At Cam's, Mr. Jackson informed Mrs. Latimer that just in case the generator didn't work—"not that I think it won't" —he'd better batten down the hatches against a storm and Mrs. Latimer replied that this was nonsense. Weathermen had been wrong before, she admitted, "but not that wrong." Mr. Jackson, however, went ahead with his precautions and she said indulgently, "You're too New England to be real, Mr. J."

Only one man had predicted a blizzard; he was an elderly amateur student of meteorology, who lived in New Jersey.

So the snow came, silent as fog, or the falling of a rose

petal. By morning the fall, which was eventually to measure over three feet, was considerable. Katie called the office. Flo was there alone, and she was going home. "Thank heaven," she said, "I can walk."

Jeremy went to work in hip boots, normally part of his fishing gear, sweaters, a windbreaker with big pockets, and a knitted wool toque. He took off after he'd shoveled the porches, steps and walks to the best of his ability for Olive and themselves.

"You'll have a heart attack," cried Katie from the kitchen door and he said, "Not me, heartless fellow that I am."

"Don't go, Jeremy," said Katie. "There won't be any customers."

"Probably no one will be there but me," said Jeremy, "but it will give me a chance to catch up on paper work. Don't worry, I'll come home if it gets worse."

No school. The twins were beside themselves with delight. Lancelot rolled deliriously in the snow and Olive got to Katie's, demanding, "Whatever will happen to Frank? He's out on the road somewhere."

"Maybe it isn't snowing there," said Katie. "Come in and have some coffee. It will stop snowing, by noon," she said optimistically.

"Are you nuts? The radio says all day and all night!"

It got worse. No Jeremy. The electric power went off and Katie's little house—like most houses except those with generators—was cold as the North Pole. Katie found some oil lamps and deplored the lack of a fireplace. She waited for Jeremy. He didn't come. Perhaps he'd started home, fallen and frozen to death. There was a wild wicked wind, as in any bonafide blizzard, and the snow drifted with it.

The telephone was still operable. She called the shop. No answer.

For lunch, a sandwich and a soft drink. She wrapped herself in blankets and thought of Susy and Roger in Hawaii. She also thought: Perhaps I should call the police and report Jeremy missing?

She worked herself into a growing panic: saw herself widowed, alone forever. She walked the floor, which was cold. She lay down again on the sofa and heard Olive screaming at the boys and Lancelot. Doors slammed and then Olive phoned. "Jeremy home?" she asked.

"No, dammit!"

"Crawl over," said Olive. "I've got the oven on"—she cooked with gas—"and I'll give you something hot to eat and drink."

"Thanks," said Katie and meant it, "but not till I hear from Jeremy."

He telephoned sometime after two. "You all right?" he asked, and Katie said furiously, "I'm fine—just starving and freezing. Why aren't you at the shop or why aren't you here?"

"I'm at Beth Nelson's," he told her. "I've been here since noon. Can't get out. I tried to get hold of Si—he has a jeep—and Beth's driveway's impossible on foot."

"Beth's!" said Katie incredulously.

He said, "She was afraid to leave her parents this morning. She called me—she had a book she wanted me to see."

"Book!" repeated Katie hysterically and hung up.

Jeremy called back. He said, "Katie, listen . . . this book could be extremely important—it's a manusript——"

"I'm going next door to Olive's," Katie interrupted, "and if she can give me a blanket and her gas holds out, I'll sleep on the kitchen floor by the oven. Goodbye. Have fun."

She put on boots, her heaviest sweater and coat, tied a scarf around her head and struggled next door.

Olive said, "Come in. You look terrible."

"I feel terrible."

The kitchen was mercifully warm; it was also full of twins and a dog twice the size of most.

"Coffee?" asked Olive. "Take off your things and sit. The bottled gas tank was filled a couple of days ago. We'll live. . . . Where's Jeremy? He can come here too. The boys can use their sleeping bags. You and Jeremy stay here. I've lamps, and water."

"So have I," said Katie. "Thank heaven we don't have wells." She shivered and Olive asked again, "Where's Jeremy?"

Katie clashed her cup into the saucer. She said, "He's at Beth Nelson's!"

"Who's she?"

"She works for him. She lives with her parents off Foster Street, back in the woods, I believe. He went there because she had a book he wanted to see."

"You've got to be kidding," said Olive.

"I'm not."

"When's he coming home?"

"I dunno. He tried to get Si Wescott's jeep, but I guess Si's phone didn't answer. Jeremy said it's impossible to walk out of the Nelson driveway. . . . It isn't really the Nelson driveway," said Katie, "but I don't know Beth's maiden name."

Olive followed this with some difficulty. She asked, "She's divorced?"

"War widow."

"That's worse," Olive declared, then added thoughtfully, "Of course, it depends on which war."

"The most recent one," Katie said bitterly.

"When did Jeremy say he'd be home?" Olive persisted.

"He didn't. . . . I couldn't care less." Katie swore under

her breath, then burst into tears. The twins looked at her with fascinated horror. "Mrs. Palmer's crying!" they said in unison, and Lancelot crept toward her and put his great solicitous head on her knees.

Olive started to say briskly, "Boys, go upstairs or outdoors," and then remembered that upstairs was like a large freezer and outdoors, a whirling, white madness. So all she said was, "Shut up, you two. Even grownups cry sometimes. Can't you see Aunt Katie's worried about Uncle Jeremy?"

It was the first time that the Palmers had been admitted to the Elder family. The twins were impressed. And their mother ordered, "Find a game or something. Try to read, for heaven's sake, and keep that dog out from underfoot. Do you want Aunt Katie to break a leg this time?"

They didn't.

"Now," said Olive, "you can cry in peace."

Katie complied with as little noise as possible, the phone rang and Olive went to it. She said, "Yes, yes of course, she's here—Katie, it's Jeremy."

"That figures," said Katie, sniffling. "I don't want to talk to him. Tell him I'll see him next week or whenever he digs out from wherever he is. I'll put a lamp in the window—your window."

Olive, a literal lass, repeated the message, listened, and then said, "Well, if you say so," and hung up.

"He said——"

"I don't care what he said!"

Olive said patiently, "I'm only the party of the third part. He said that you are an idiot. He said he sends his love. He said you're to stay here with us as long as the fuel holds out. He said he was sure he could get Si and the jeep and if not Si, the fire department or police or someone, and be home tomorrow morning."

"We'll hire a band."

"You're being childish, honey."

"I am not. Here we have the worst storm I've seen since I was a kid, and he had to go out in it, to mind his store. Then he had to go into the woods to look at a manuscript. You'd think it was the Dead Sea Scrolls. How was I supposed to get along?"

"Men," Olive commented profoundly. "I take it this Beth person is young. She probably wears thick glasses, weighs eighty-four pounds and is dedicated to her work."

"She's dedicated," said Katie. "She's also one of the most beautiful dames I've ever seen."

"You know Jeremy wouldn't——"

"Don't be an ass," Katie implored her. "I don't think Jeremy is planning to sleep under a family eiderdown with Beth Nelson. Not now, anyway. I'm not jealous. I'm not even suspicious. I am simply so mad I could scream."

"You'll scare the twins."

"Scream, Aunt Katie," said one of them, hopefully looking up from his checker game.

Katie said, "Well, no. Too much effort. Shall we play double solitaire? How about the radio?"

Time dragged interminably. It went on snowing and became darker than the inside of a cow. Olive lit the lamps, which smoked. She coughed and said, "I'll put one in the window."

"It will catch the curtains," Katie said. "Let him come home on all fours."

They had an early, scratch supper. "I was going to shop today," Olive apologized, "but hamburger and home fries are better than nothing. Eat, Katie, and keep your strength up."

Jeremy called again and Olive said, "She's all right. Just mad and I don't blame her. . . . We've had supper. How about you? . . . Oh, I see. . . . Fireplace. . . . Katie's staying here."

She hung up and reported faithfully: "Mrs. Nelson's parents' name is Easton. They had steaks, cooked in the fireplace."

"How cozy!" said Katie.

"He'll be home soon as he gets hold of our busy landlord."

Katie went to bed under half a dozen blankets. Olive offered her a sleeping pill, saying, "You may as well take one, I shall; that way we won't know it when we freeze to death. The boys will be better off in sleeping bags in the kitchen. Of course, they could suffocate."

The phone rang. It was Frank calling from a distant town. Was Olive all right, And the boys? He'd managed to get the last room in what he termed a god-forsaken motel. But there was food, drink and warmth. Yes, a generator. "When we buy a house," he added, "we'll also buy a generator."

"Katie's here," said Olive.

"Good. Where's Jeremy?"

"In the village. He couldn't get home. Forgot his skis," Olive told him, laughing. "Take it easy tomorrow if you get out of there."

Katie said, later, "You know, Jeremy has skis. I don't suppose he even thought of taking them."

"What man ever thinks?" asked Olive.

In the morning Si's jeep roared up Baker Street while Katie and Olive were having coffee. It had ceased to snow. The sun was brilliant; it was a dazzling white day, with pale blue sky, laden trees. Katie heard Jeremy say, "Thanks, Si," and clump around through the snow to Olive's back steps.

"Come in," suggested Olive. "Have coffee. You look great."

"I feel great. Made the discovery of a century—or almost. . . . Hi, Katie!"

"Good morning," said Katie politely. "I trust you passed a comfortable night."

"She's still mad," Olive explained unnecessarily.

"Of course. She's female." He draped a cold soggy arm around his wife and suggested, "Suppose we stay here for a while and keep warm. The power is expected to be on shortly, at least in our end of town. Later, after I'm sure you're all right, I'll look in at the shop—unless the police call me earlier."

"Police?" asked Katie. "You've committed a crime or something?"

"Not yet. But there's been vandalism in the village. Kids on skis early this morning, after the snow stopped. They had flashlights, and broke into some of the shops—stationery, sporting goods, the Howard Street Diner, to name a few. The police were busy all night with emergencies—getting the ambulance through to the hospital, for instance. And there were accidents and fires. So it wasn't discovered until daylight. They haven't reported that the bookshop was entered, but I'd like to take a look."

"First things first," agreed Katie too amiably. "Are you skiing to Colonial Way?"

"It's an idea. I didn't think of my skis until late last night."

"Too busy, no doubt," remarked his wife.

Olive, fearing an explosion, interjected, "Stick around, gang, I can offer pasta for lunch."

15

✳✳✳✳ The power was restored to Colonial Way and the area and as far as Baker Street by noon. Katie and Jeremy returned home, with a large bowl of Olive's macaroni and cheese and a thermos of coffee. "In case it goes off again," Olive said. "Come back if it does."

She was considerably relieved to see them go. She loved her neighbors, but she couldn't endure further the politely hostile chitchat between them. She thought: Thank God, Frank and I yell at each other; it clears the atmosphere. Her half house had become, after Jeremy's entrance, a couple of sizes too small.

Jeremy, carrying lunch, trudged through the snow and up the steps. "Be careful," he warned and Katie said, "I'm doing just fine."

Their house was very cold, but it would soon warm up; the furnace was roaring away and Jeremy said from the kitchen, "Even if the power goes off again, the heat will hold. I've turned up the thermostat."

"That's logical," Katie agreed, heading for the stairs.

"Where are you going?" he inquired. "Let's eat."

"I'm not hungry."

"Okay," said Jeremy evenly. "I'll eat and look over the skis after I've locked up the manuscript. . . . Actually it's a series of small diaries," he informed her hopefully.

Katie was shedding her outer garments. She'd left the boots in the kitchen. "I have to phone Flo, and I want to check with Linda and Mrs. Latimer," she said.

"I'll put the macaroni in the oven to keep it warm in case you change your mind," Jeremy told her.

He ate alone at the kitchen table and heard Katie telephoning from their bedroom. He thought: She has a point of course, poor kid! Good thing she could get next door. But this continuing attitude of resentment was childish.

He told her so when, after a considerable length of time, she came downstairs, decided she could manage a spoonful of food, and cleaned up the rest of Olive's generous donation. Jeremy, meanwhile, locked up the diaries in his desk drawer in the study, and found his skis in the cluttered hall closet.

He said pleasantly, "Katie, you are being childish."

"Olive thinks so too."

"Why? Didn't you believe me?"

"Of course I believed you. Don't be stupid. You couldn't make that up. If you'd wanted to enjoy a weather watch with Beth Nelson, you could easily have thought of something better than 'She had a book she wanted me to see.' I'm childish, sure and I'm mad because you went to work yesterday morning when there wasn't a chance of a customer, and your help had no intention of coming out. So I don't hear from you, the shop's phone doesn't answer and you go off to look at a book and can't get back. If Olive hadn't been next door, I'd have frozen or starved—well, just pneumonia perhaps. You're inconsiderate and unkind and I was worried sick over you."

"Katie darling, don't cry. And I'm so sorry."

"I'm not crying," said Katie, the tears running down a face as guiltless of makeup as a five-year-old's, "and being sorry isn't much help."

He picked her up from her chair, carried her into the living room and sat down with an armful of half-weeping, wholly inimical wife. He said, "Quit struggling. I'm home. Everything's all right."

"How too masculine!" said Katie, ceasing to struggle. "Jeremy, when the shop didn't answer, I thought you'd fallen, and were injured or freezing."

"I said I was sorry. I am. I'm hooked on the diaries." He waited and this time she asked, in a small, reluctant voice, "What diaries?"

"Beth turned them up. She's still cleaning the old aunt's attic. They were in the bottom of a trunk she'd overlooked. Seems there's an ancestress in the Easton family, who was married to a Captain in the Revolution, from this state. He was a silversmith—no threat to Paul Revere, but a good one. The Eastons have a little box he made, very unlike the English work of that period and unusual in that it's evidently a patch box and the women of that era in the Colonies didn't wear patches, normally. Anyway, he went off to war, and his brother, a surgeon, with him. The silversmith's wife kept diaries. Her name was Charity Easton. Parts of the diaries are a little hard to decipher, although she wrote a clear hand. She was a natural; she liked detail; she copied letters from her husband and brother-in-law—the latter was killed. She wrote of the town, the people, the marriages, births and deaths and the gossip. It's all hardship and courage, anxiety and optimism, depression and scandal. It needs editing, but that won't be difficult. Beth and her parents have given me permission——"

"And the aunt?"

"No problem." He gave her a tremendous squeeze. "Maybe you'd like to hear bits and pieces? We'll work on it here," he announced.

"We?"

"Beth and I."

"Oh," said Katie, not resigned to long evenings with Jeremy and his collaborator shut in the study while she read or listened to radio next door or in bed.

He said, "It's a very exciting challenge. Other diaries have been published of course, relating to that era, but there's something special here—the woman's viewpoint. And Charity Easton was a brilliant observer of customs, manners, morals—"

"What will you do with it?"

"We'll type it and then Beth and I will edit. Then we'll talk to publishers. The money, if it's accepted, would be a godsend to the Eastons, especially to the ancient aunt in the nursing home."

"What's in it for you?" Katie inquired and he looked at her in astonishment.

"My name," he said, "I assume, along with Beth's. Nothing more except my time and the joy of bringing Charity's refreshing outlook on her life and times to the reading public. She was, incidentally, almost three hundred years ahead of her time in her attitude toward her own sex. She was bucking for liberation from kitchen, children and domineering husbands, which makes it pretty relevant. And the picture emerges, through the pages of a young, pretty woman, deeply in love with, and afraid, for her guy, involved with the war, and with her town. It should make a book club—it should make everything. I think there's even a movie in it."

"Hold 'em, Newt, they're rearing."

"Oh, sure. I should know the obstacles if anyone does," he granted.

"You know a lot of publishers."

"By reputation, most of them. Usually I see only their salesmen. I've only met a couple of editors. Cam can be a big help, however——"

"Cam? Why?"

"He owns a big block of stock in Mason, Jackson and Demerest, Inc. It's one of the biggest firms in the country——"

"Then Beth Nelson has three things going for her," Katie decided, "you, Cam, and her ancestress."

"That's right. We'll all do our best. I hope Charity takes a good look from where she is now and makes a helpful suggestion now and then."

"You sound like Jessica!"

"Jessica has something going for her too. Wish I had," Jeremy said.

But Katie's mind had leaped away. "Linda and Tom are fine," she announced, looking at Jeremy critically. "You didn't even ask me what she said when I telephoned."

"I was too busy dodging missiles."

She thought: I am uptight. Not enough to see Ben again, but I still cry a lot. It's scary.

"Okay," she agreed. "Well, Tom got to work and Ella—you know, the old girl who works for them—came on, of all things, her grandson's sled. He's a big boy, she's a little woman, so he dragged her to work. Linda wasn't scared. She said, 'If I'd been pregnant, I'd have been terrified. I'm

143

not scared of anything now, except of something happening to Tom.' "

"Linda's remarkable," Jeremy commented. "She has stamina, and the ability to adjust. I'm glad. She'll get well and have a couple of babies. You'll see."

"Twins?"

"One at a time. Look at poor Olive, what she goes through with her duplicates. Did you get Mrs. Latimer?"

"I did. She was in a state, absolutely livid about Mr. Jackson, the indispensable handy man."

"Why? Don't tell me that he made a pass at her? She'd cut his throat."

"No, she wouldn't; she'd evade—but like it. Seems he told her there was a blizzard brewing. She didn't believe him. He went right ahead making all preparations in case something went wrong with the generator—it runs on gasoline—and he had a five-gallon can, but he said, you can't ever be sure, even though he ran it weekly to keep the battery up."

"She should be glad Jackson's cautious."

"She's annoyed because he was right. Also, I think that she believes in her role as a resourceful British female. Stiff upper lip, heave to, do the work, cope like crazy. . . . Oh and she told me that, about ten days ago, Ronnie ran away from school."

"Where to?"

"She didn't get far. Her explanation was she was bored. Her mother fell apart and called Mrs. Latimer. Cam was on the Coast."

"She'll run away frequently; they'd better get used to it," Jeremy prophesied.

"Remember how when she came here she'd drag up a chair and say 'Talk time'?"

"I remember."

"Well," said Katie, "maybe she ran out of people to talk to."

"For a young woman who doesn't know anything about kids, you astonish me."

"I was thinking of myself. I ran away a couple of times. Sheer boredom."

"I'd better keep an eye on you."

"Not necessary. I'm rarely bored now. Oh, when I creamed my ankle, of course, but that was cabin fever. . . . Do you suppose the mail will come?"

"Tomorrow. Maybe even late today. Why?"

"I thought I'd hear from Mother. That one postal all palms and hula girls is all we've had."

Jeremy rose. He said, "Well, go do some housework; or listen to your DJs. I'm off—on skis."

"How long since you've skied? You haven't since we were married."

"Oh, it's a while, but I'll manage. It's hardly uphill to Colonial Way."

"You could break a leg."

"Naturally. So keep your fingers crossed. I'll try not to make any sitz marks."

"But, traffic—"

"My dearest Katie, there isn't any; or, very little. We're still snowed in. If the power goes off again, phone me."

"Why should it? You keep saying that and Olive too."

"Trees falling, branches, someone skidding into something. See you. Incidentally, is there anything for supper? Nothing will be open this afternoon, except maybe the delicatessen; they don't miss many chances. They were robbed too, but not of everything."

Katie said, "There's chicken in the freezer. I'll cope."

"With my assistance." He kissed her and she went to the back door to watch him put on his skis.

"That damned shop!" she said to herself as he started down the path. "Jeremy," she called, her small face rosy in the wind.

He looked over his shoulder. "What's wrong?"

"Nothing. Did Charity ever have children?"

"Who?" he asked astonished. "Oh, Charity. One baby after her Captain went soldiering. A boy. It died. After his return, two or more. She takes us into their life after the war. After the second child, she stopped keeping journals."

"Too busy, poor woman," Katie diagnosed.

"Get back into the house, you're turning blue," he said, laughing, and took off, skillfully enough.

Katie, shivering, returned to warmth and comfort. She was smiling. She'd showed interest in Charity and thought it handsome of her, because she wasn't really interested. Well, a little . . . enough to have an excuse to interrupt Beth and Jeremy at their editing. She thought: The study isn't big enough for two typewriters. I suppose they'll make room and bring in a table. The noise will be appalling.

She took the chicken parts from the freezer, went into the living room and settled herself on the couch. If the power did go off, she supposed they'd have to go to Olive's or into the village to some place where it was still on. Maybe the Bankses, maybe Si Wescott's, or maybe Flo's. She told herself optimistically: "It can't go off again."

Later, it did so for a short time. She called Jeremy and he said, "Someone from the power company has just been here. They're working on branches fallen from weight and wind. If it isn't back within an hour, go to Olive's."

"Jeremy, you're all right? You didn't fall or anything?"

"I fall," he replied austerely, "only for ravishing women."

Which reminded her. "Did Beth come in?" she asked, elaborately casual.

"No. . . . I'll be home in a couple of hours. Take it easy."

Katie watched the clock. She called the Bankses and Jessica reported that their power was still off, so Gordon was shoveling coal. "This big old house has a coal furnace, installed early in World War Two and still operable. There's been coal here in a huge bin ever since," she said. "Rosie Niles is here; her entire house is electric. She wants to speak to you."

"Hi," said Rosie cheerfully. "Isn't it wonderful—the joy of living in the country? It's like a marriage: when it works, it's fine. I'd like to see you, Katie, once we're back to more or less normal. I'll call you."

"I would have thought you'd go to the city."

"The city's in a bad way too, people skiing down various avenues, everyone screaming at whatever removes snow—sanitation department or something. Besides, I'm safer here with Jessica to keep an eye on me."

Olive called. She said, "Well, here we go again. Come over. Where's Jeremy?"

"He skied off to the shop."

"We saw him go. I can offer you the usual hospitality. If you've looked out recently, you saw the boys and their great animal. I've got them in now, drying in front of the oven."

"Thanks," said Katie, "you're a lamb. But Jeremy says he expects the power will be on again shortly. If not, I'll be at your back door."

It was cold and it was lonely. Thank God for the telephone. She supposed some lines were out, but not theirs. She called Amy Irvington.

"You and Benjy all right?" she asked.

"Fine. We went to Ben's parents yesterday and stayed for the night. They have a generator. Our power was restored this morning. Ben got to the hospital and he's there now."

"What about the office?"

"Yesterday, no patients. Okay today."

The power came on. Jeremy came home and the minor crisis was over.

16

✳✳✳✳ Little Oxford dug itself out. Power came on, went off, and was erratic for a time. Otherwise everything was normal. The bookshop prospered as people decided if they were to have more storms, they'd better stock up with books, hard cover, paperback, lending library. "Though, of course," said a client of Katie's thoughtfully, "if you've a clutch from the lending library, you could be stuck with overtime. Little Oxford Library too."

The liquor stores were merry with the ringing of cash registers. This had been a short period of inconvenience, but there were storms in the West, Midwest and North which lasted for days. "Don't get caught with your Scotch down," customers admonished themselves. Didn't storms come from west to east?

Sporting goods shops showed a profit in skis and other items. Mr. Jackson broke into his piggy bank and bought snowshoes. He asked Mrs. Latimer, "You skate, mam?"

"I used to," she said, "back home."

"Get yourself a pair. Good skating in the Village Park, after we've had week or two of zero."

"We couldn't!"

"We do. There's skating too on that there lake, a mile or so from here. Do you good. You look peaked."

People laid in more Irish sweaters, great scarves, heavy slacks, windbreakers, and mittens. Several shopkeepers went home and said to their wives, "Been such a mild winter I began to figure on early sales, but everything's booming. We could get off to Florida for a couple of weeks this spring, maybe."

In the Palmers' half house on Baker Street—Jeremy had threatened to put up a sign reading 221 B when they first went there—things were not normal as far as Katie was concerned. Every evening after supper the redheaded Mrs. Nelson came to work on the Easton journals. Now and then she ate with the Palmers. Jeremy had cleared out the study to some extent. The TV set was now in the living room, the books off the floor, chairs moved; and he'd brought from the shop a small extra table. Typewriters clattered. Beth took one diary, he took another; there were six in all. After the typing, they began the editing which, Katie feared, might take them into July. Once she asked, "Why don't you two just talk into dictaphones and have it all transcribed?"

"Costs too much," said Jeremy.

And Beth said, "I'm an emotional reader. I laugh and cry, and there's a lot here to laugh and cry over. I used to read to Kim," she continued reflectively, "the short time we were together. He'd fall asleep and I'd start crying and wake him up." She looked away, across the room, and her mind, behind the lovely eyes, was not in Little Oxford.

Katie thought with considerable rancor: Isn't it ridiculous? I actually like her!

This preoccupation with Charity curtailed the Palmers' social life. Jeremy couldn't go out evenings except when Beth, because of one obligation or another toward her parents, couldn't come, and even then he went with reluctance; he'd rather stay home and work alone.

Now and then, after Beth had gone home, he'd read a little to Katie. Against her will she found her interest awakened and growing as Charity Easton began to assume for her the reality she had had all long for her devoted editors.

Then Cam came back to Little Oxford. On his brief trip to England, he'd picked up a stubborn virus. So he took time off and returned to his house and Mrs. Latimer's nursing and spoiling. The women who helped her in the house were ordered to walk softly, shut off their radios if any, as well as the kitchen TV and set up trays on which Mrs. Latimer planned to serve small portions of delicious and nourishing invalid food.

When Cam was better, against Mrs. Latimer's express wishes he had a delighted Mr. Jackson take him to Baker Street. Mr. Jackson had never before been privileged to drive the Mercedes Benz beyond moving it in or out of the garage. "Come back in an hour, Jackson," said Cam.

He'd phoned Jeremy. Could he come to see them? He was indescribably bored.

So he came and Beth was there, of course, as he probably knew she would be.

"My cup runneth over, literally," Katie remarked to herself, spilling coffee.

But Beth was helpful in Katie's kitchen, never in the way, quiet, efficient and, Katie had discovered, a good cook. One evening when Katie had come home tired, the clients all having been difficult, Beth had said, "If you'll just show me where things are, Katie . . . Jeremy's sort of lost in the Revolution, I think. What do you want for supper?"

At any rate, after Cam had been there for an hour, reading Beth's meticulous and Jeremy's erratic typing he asked, "Use your phone?" and called Mr. Jackson, who was comfortable with Mrs. Latimer in the kitchen.

"Never mind coming back now," he said and Katie thought with horror: He isn't spending the night, is he, for pete's sake? But she was soothed to hear him add, "I'll phone when I want to go home. . . . Yes, of course, put her on." He waited and then spoke to Mrs. Latimer. He said, after a few minutes, "I'm a better judge of my strength than you are, Polly. Stop being Mary Poppins or whatever Nanny you are at the moment. I grew up a long time ago."

Cam was extremely enthusiastic about the Easton diaries. When they were ready, after the editing—"and retyping," said Jeremy gloomily—he'd talk to Mason. "He's the history and nonfiction buff in the firm," Cam said.

He went home just before midnight, and after Beth had gone. Before she went, she helped wash cups, saucers and the glasses they'd used to toast Charity. Katie had also made sandwiches.

Upstairs, finally, Katie said sleepily, "I'm half dead. I'm still involved with Mrs. Morrison."

"Who?"

"Isn't it whom? . . . I told you about her. She's looking for a summer rental."

" 'If winter comes . . .' " Jeremy began, undressing.

"Never mind the quotations. The woman's a menace. Lots of people look for summer rentals during the winter, sometimes with options to buy. I've shown her half a dozen houses; she hates them all, but is determined to come here. She wants a swimming pool outside, 'help laid on,' as Mrs. Latimer might say, and within walking distance of the shops. It isn't easy. Also, she has three children, four dogs and two cats. That's not easy either. Most people who go off to Spain or wherever, and want to rent for part or full season, specify no pets, and some don't want children."

Jeremy wasn't listening. He was looking into the mirror as if he could see there his reflected fate.

"Jeremy!"

"What?"

"You could at least pretend to listen and even be a little interested."

"I'm sorry, Katie. I apologize."

"Forget it. I know you're thinking of the diaries."

"That's right. Cam is extremely taken with what he's read so far."

"Oh, sure!" said Katie. "Also with Beth."

He turned from the mirror. "Well, possibly," he admitted, "but not entirely. Cam has good judgment; also he's a businessman."

"But he wouldn't profit from them?"

"If the publishers do, he will," said her husband. "He invested in the firm because it's sound and reputable and has been for almost a century. If they invest in the Easton diaries, they'll do a good P.R. job." He laughed. "Beth may even find herself on talk shows," he added, amused.

"How about you?"

"Perish forbid. Anyway, if it's as good as we think it is no one loses."

One bright, bitter-cold afternoon, Rosie Niles came into the Warner office, smiled at Flo, and asked, "Mrs. Palmer busy?"

"No," answered Flo, wondering if she should rise and curtsy to the legendary Mrs. Niles whom she'd seen only a few times on the street.

"I telephoned a while ago . . ." Rosie began. Flo said, "Yes, Mrs. Niles," and Rosie asked, "What's your name, as long as you know mine?"

"Florence Sawyer," Flo told her and Rosie said, "Bet they call you Flo," and Flo nodded. "Mine's Roscika," said Rosie, "so you know what they call me."

Flo laughed and signaled Katie on the intercom. "Mrs. Niles is here," she said in a rather hushed voice.

Rosie went into Katie's office, remarking, "You said you wouldn't be busy."

"I'm not. It's mostly paper work." She looked at Rosie and smiled, "Putting your house on the market?" she inquired hopefully.

"No. I have to have a place in which I can sulk or scream, and not disturb neighbors. Whenever I leave it, I come back to it as to a shelter and lick my wounds, if any. I've been in town for a spell. You know about the boy Jessica discovered for me? He has the makings, a superb voice," said Rosie. "But it needs training. I've got him that. Now I've come to take you home with me. For tea, and I mean tea unless you'd prefer coffee. I've been promising myself I'd see you, ever since Christmas."

"I like that," Katie said, smiling.

How pretty she is! Rosie thought. Unartificial, delightful; the contrast between her hair and eyes. But a little tense. . . . Rosie knew tension when she saw it.

Aloud, she said, "I'll sit here and admire you while you do anything necessary."

"Just a couple of calls, then I'm free for the rest of the day. Business isn't exactly brisk, though some trickles in. Mrs. Warner's on a cruise, and none of the rest of us have learned how to stir things up."

"I know Emily Warner," said Rosie, smiling. "She's a real

stirrer-upper. She's been trying for some years to bulldoze me into selling my house. She promised a fantastic price."

Katie made her calls. Rosie listened, smoking, using the pristine ashtray. She thought: But this kid's a go-getter too, in a different way from La Warner's drive, I'll bet anything in my safe deposit.

When Katie hung up, Rosie asked, "You don't sing, do you?"

"Good grief," answered Katie, startled. "Not even a sour note. I can't carry a tune, really, except in my head."

"Pity. You're not too old to be trained and you'd have everything else going for you—appearance, personality, vitality and," said Rosie casually, "ambition."

"Ambition!"

"I sense it; the vibes, as the kids say. Do you like music?"

"I love it, mostly pop," said Katie without apology. "I listen by the hour. Poor Jeremy suffers, if he's home. He's a classical buff and knows a lot, too."

"He's a dream, your Jeremy," said Rosie. "Where's your car?"

"Parked off Parson's Hill."

"We'll take mine. The Village isn't exactly crowded today. I'm a shop's length up street."

They said goodbye to Flo. "You can reach me at Mrs. Niles' for a while," Katie told her, "and then home, if anything comes up."

Rosie's car was long, low and expensive, also very comfortable. "Nervous when someone else drives?" Rosie asked.

"Occasionally; Cam for instance, but not Jeremy, or," added Katie mildly astonished, "you."

"I'm a damned good driver when I'm sober," Rosie announced casually, "and I'm sober most of the time; well, in a sense all the time. When I get the unbeatable urge, I head for a place called Quiet House. It's run by what's known erroneously as ex-alcoholics and is connected with AA. It's not a place where they dry you out, but one to which you go when you're scared. You get good food and they see that you eat it, and there's a sort of undemanding occupational therapy. I actually learned to do crewel work there. I'm rather good at it too. You have very mild sedation to help you sleep, and companionship—around the clock. If you start going up the walls, someone's there. They talk with you, they listen and they pray with you. They quite literally hold your hand. They lift you over the hump and send you home. I knew about it vaguely—there are lots of such retreats over the country. Bing knew more than I. He sent me there, so he no longer has to toss me into a hospital or sanitarium. Works fine so far, for me," said Rosie cheerfully.

Katie had seen the Niles house from a distance. It was contemporary, glass, exotic woods, sun decks, land. The pool, Rosie explained, was around back. "Incidentally, if it's ever summer again, feel free to use it anytime," she told Katie.

"Then we'll have two," said Katie happily, "yours and Cam's."

An erect elderly man was riding herd over a couple of husky young gentlemen with long hair flowing down from under woolen caps, who were cleaning walks, chopping at ice.

"Jabez," said Rosie, "this is Mrs. Palmer. Jabez Hunt," she told Katie, "my right and left hands. Lives over the garage and never sleeps."

"Don't pay her no heed," said Jabez to Katie. "Palmer?" His lean face was illuminated briefly. "Related to the Palmer bookshop?"

"I'm the bookshop's wife."

"He's all right," said Jabez. "I read a lot, mostly about history. I go in, he tells me what's new, even lends me old books. I get Westerns too—I like a change—from the lending library. Me and Mr. Palmer, we talk a lot. Never too busy, he is."

Rosie took her guest into the house and they were met by a striking young woman who took their wraps. "Tea," said Rosie, "in the living room. . . . Your mother feeling better, Irma?"

"She says she's fine, Mrs. Niles."

"Suppose you manage supper, and keep your mother in bed. If she hasn't shaken that cold by tomorrow, I'll call Doctor Irvington."

The living room was vast; the furniture looked as if it had been created by someone in the Inquisition, but it was extremely comfortable. There were paintings, and Katie, wandering about, looked at them, exclaiming over a Chinese ornament or crewel-work pillows.

"I collect a little," Rosie said, following her, "mostly young artists with talent who need encouragement. . . . Come into the library."

Hi fi, and dozens of framed photographs on tables and the walls, many of them signed. Rosie said, "Nostalgia Alley. I spend a great deal of time in here. You knew I was married to Bill Niles and sang with his band and in supper clubs?" Katie nodded and Rosie said, "Here's his picture, one of them."

"He was very good-looking," Katie said.

"A beautiful guy," said Rosie. "Also a steamroller of a perfectionist, I guess you'd call it. The big band sound has come back. I have the old records and now the new, and I listen. Sometimes it tears me up, which is stupid. I'd rather listen than read." She waved her small paw. "All those books," she said. "Bill liked books, so we had them scattered all over the place, even traveling and in hotels. I buy books now and then, too."

Back in the living room they shared an elegant imported tea and tiny sandwiches and Katie said, sighing, "This is a marvelous house."

"The house I was born in," Rosie said, "stood here, but nearer the road. I tore it down and built and came back now and then from Europe, the Orient, God knows where. Jabez caretook. But when I decided to live here, Bing persuaded me I couldn't be alone. So there's Jabez, of course, and the three-times-a-week gardener in season, and in the house a couple, a good, loyal woman—Addie and her daughter, Irma. I suspect we'll lose Irma one of these days to the young man who comes calling and with whom she tears around on a motorbike on her days off. Addie lives in a constant state of foreboding. But there'll be someone else if Irma marries. Addie has a niece Myra who used to work for me occasionally. She's not married nor likely to be. We'll see. A step at a time. I've learned that with some difficulty—one day, one step. When I plan ahead, it isn't for me."

Katie asked, "Didn't I hear something about a young man and his voice?"

"Yes. First there was a kid—Joyce Kally—she was in school; her parents were dead. She lived with her grandparents who were conscious of their responsibility and very strict. I persuaded them—with Jessica Banks' help—to let me start her voice training. When she was through school—she wouldn't hear of college—I took her abroad, found her the right teacher and living quarters with a French family to whom she became attached. Madame was a busty, busy Tartar with a small mustache. She knew where Joyce was every minute of the day and night. I've been over to see her several times. She was in student concerts. I flew her home when her grandmother was dying. The grandfather's in a nursing home now, and the little house is sold, so Joyce has that money."

I bet you pay for Grandpa, Katie thought and looked at her hostess with admiration and respect.

"Joyce will be back for good in another year. She'd like to live in one of those excellent clubs for girl students. I've a flat in the city. We'll work it out. She'll be ready for auditioning, and she'll go on studying. Women's organizations make a good start. They get fair publicity."

"You do so much good," Katie said.

"Who knows, maybe she'd be better off living here, getting married, raising kids, singing lullabies, joining her church choir. But I'm selfish. It's been such fun, and now I have an interest. Joyce, this new boy, and others I hope. I have Jessica Banks to thank. . . . She looks as fragile as a flower, and she's gentle as a lovely summer day, but as strong as a rock. I must have read that somewhere," she added, astonished. "I couldn't have made it up!"

Katie said, "I'm sort of scared of her—she—well—she knows so much."

"Mostly we call it hunches," Rosie said, laughing. "But don't go against them. . . . Jeremy's related to her, isn't he?"

"Yes. I wish I knew her better."

"Just give her a chance, honey."

Later, Rosie asked, over her cigarette, "You and Jeremy getting along all right? Hey, don't look so shocked. I'm not a lady. I'm just interested and I like you both."

Katie said, opening her mind, "Most of the time."

"That's a good percentage. Bill and I did, too. I guess the thing to remember is deference—for each other's hangups, opinions and whatever goes on inside every human being, in solitude. No friend, lover, husband, wife, parent—no one can penetrate another's inner solitude. It's damned difficult to learn that. Bill had learned—he was always a faster student than I—but I was learning . . . when he was killed. Did you know I remarried, twice?"

"I'd heard." Now Katie cast gentility aside. "Why?" she inquired.

"Good question, but not the sixty-four-thousand one. You have dollar signs, as well as question marks, in your big eyes. Not money, my dear. I had all I needed. Companionship, I thought—a little sex. That was for the birds. My husbands— or episodes, as I think of them of them—were disappointed in me. Sure I was younger, giddy and outgoing, but also, smashed, much of the time."

Katie said on an impulse unusual for her, "I think you're great."

"Thanks. Now we'll get going. My new protégé is coming after early supper for a workout. I find I can teach—well— just basics. I'll take you back to your car, Katie."

On the way, she said, "You and Jeremy should consider having a couple of kids."

"We have considered."

"And . . . ?"

"He says yes, I say no. Not yet. I like my job. I'm interested in it and good at it," Katie told her, "and I want to be free for a while longer."

"Don't let it go too long," Rosie advised. "If Bill and I had had children things might have been different after he was killed. Not that I'm at all sure; there are plenty of alcoholic mothers. That's why I won't adopt Joyce. I don't think I'm stable enough."

Rosie, after she'd taken Katie to the parking lot, returned to Colonial Way, parked in front of the bookshop, rushed in and said, "Hi, Jeremy, your wife's on her way home."

"From where? . . . You're looking pretty sharp."

"From my hovel. We had tea and what is disgustingly known as girl talk. Look after her. Tell her I dropped in to inform on her and also, for the love of God, tell her to call me Rosie. I forgot."

On the way out she spoke to Beth Nelson, asking, "Up to anything special?"

Jeremy was right behind her. He said, "Stay three more minutes and I'll tell all." He dragged her into the office, beckoned to Beth. "Beth has these diaries . . ." he began.

Rosie listened. She said, "Sounds good potentially. Need any financing?"

"No, thank you. We'll let the publishers do that," he told her. "Cam has a very good lead. I've a few. It's hard work but great fun."

Rosie said, "Good luck. I'll buy fifty copies when it comes out. Can't promise to read it though."

Headed home, she thought: those two working together? Well, no wonder Katie's uptight. But it's a little early in the marriage for either of them to start looking elsewhere, given the sort of people they are. Cam's interest doesn't surprise me. Rosie had a wicked little grin which she now employed. She said to herself: "I'll give anyone fifty to one that Cam gets them a publisher, and himself a gorgeous wife, as I doubt that young Mrs. Nelson would settle for anything less than a legalized relationship."

17

✳✳✳✳ Jeremy came home shortly and Katie asked, "What do you want for supper? Chops?"

Instead of inquiring, "What else is available?" he said, "Nothing, I feel terrible."

"You coming down with something?" she asked and felt a little stab of apprehension. Jeremy, during all the time she'd known him, had rarely been ill. Oh, now and then a headache, occasionally a cold.

"I certainly hope not. . . . You fix something for yourself. I'll make you a drink."

"I'll call Ben," she said instantly.

He countered, on a note of irritation, "Ben's busy. Forget it. I'll go to bed and be fine tomorrow. I told Beth she could stop by and pick up the journal she's been working on and go on with it at home. She has a typewriter there."

Katie went into the study. He brought her a drink, and sat down, heavily for him, and Katie said anxiously, "There are all sorts of viruses going around."

"I'm aware of that. Mary Hawkes is out sick and one of

the kids in the stock room who comes after school. Virus? Everything's a virus, now, from athlete's foot to a zymotic disease."

"What on earth is that?"

"Just a disease, only appropriate thing I could think of beginning with z."

"No wonder you're so revoltingly brilliant at Scrabble."

He wasn't laughing. He said, "Well, Beth can take over; she's capable enough. Brother, do I feel zapped. And that's another z," he reminded her, trying to smile.

"Jeremy, please go up to bed." She put down her glass and went over to touch his forehead. "You've a temperature," she said.

"That's right. Get away from me," he ordered and she returned to her chair, thinking: I'm frightened.

"Go broil a chop," he suggested fretfully. "You have to eat and if you say you aren't hungry"—a look of distaste crossed his face at the thought of food—"I'll strangle you."

"You go to bed."

"I'll stay up until Beth comes."

He leaned his head against the back of his chair and seemed to sleep. Katie sat there, looking at him. She thought: I'm useless. I'm terrified of illness. I have no skill at nursing. She thought of Linda who would take care of anything—a sick dog or cat, her friends, Tom. . . . I wish Mother were here, she thought further . . . or someone.

Someone came. It was Beth Nelson; Katie heard her come up the steps and ran to the door. She said, "Jeremy's ill, Beth, really ill."

"I know. Doctor Irvington has put Mary in the hospital. I called tonight just before I left the shop; her sister told me." She went in and Jeremy opened over-bright eyes. He said, "Stay away from me, Beth."

"I shall."

"Now that you're here, I'll go to bed. Take the diary—and take over the shop. . . . How's Mary?"

"She's pretty sick," Beth reported, "but she'll be all right. This appears to be a sudden savage but brief bug." She looked warningly at Katie and Katie thought: She won't tell him about the hospital.

Jeremy got to his feet. On the way to the stairs, he said, "I'll sleep in the guest room. Beth, make Katie eat something. If she gets run down . . ." His voice trailed off, and the two women stood regarding each other.

"Into the kitchen," said Beth. "He's the boss. What do you fancy?"

"Nothing, yet in a way I'm hungry. Empty perhaps. I'd taken a couple of chops out of the freezer."

"Bring your glass and follow me," Beth said, adding, when Katie tried to be helpful, "Get out of the way, Katie. I'm a demon in the kitchen. Like the legendary Garbo, I want to be alone. Or almost."

Katie sat at the kitchen table and watched Beth—sure of herself, easy, saving steps, washing up as she went along. Just the kind of woman Jeremy should have married, she thought, gloomily. She has everything.

Presently the chop, a salad, fruit and coffee were ready. "Eat," said Beth sternly, and Katie said, "If I had a long tail, I'd wag it. . . . Did Jeremy seem ill at the shop? He was all right this morning."

"Not until just before he went home, about the time Mrs. Niles came in. I thought he was making an effort when he talked to her——"

"What we need here," said Katie, "is Martha Hudson."

"Do I know her?"

"Not unless Jeremy's infected you with his Sherlock Holmes mania. She was Sherlock's and Doctor Watson's housekeeper. I guess we also need Florence Nightingale."

Beth smiled. She said, "I'd forgotten about Jeremy's Sherlock. I don't read mysteries, even the old ones. I hate violence of any kind, especially since the war. . . . Look, I'll wash up; you go and sit with Jeremy. I'll pick up the Journal and let myself out. Don't worry too much," she said gently. "Jeremy's a strong, healthy man."

Katie, docilely going up stairs, thought with a small sense of triumph: They may share the bookshop interest and Beth's Charity, but not Sherlock. . . .

She found Jeremy safely in bed and he opened one eye. "Beth?" he asked.

"She fixed supper for me," said Katie, "and she's about to go home. She'll look after things at the shop."

"Katie, go to bed. I took aspirin. I'll be all right. And don't keep popping in and out of here. I can't have you laid up and me not able to look after you, and if Beth gets it——"

"She won't," Katie assured him, feeling certain of her statement.

"Someone has to mind the store," he said sleepily and Katie thought: If this bug is raging through Little Oxford like gypsy moth caterpillars in season, the shop can just close its doors.

She said, "Darling, try to sleep. I'll leave our door open."

But she closed it temporarily after she reached the bedroom, which, suddenly looked extremely empty and much larger than usual. Then she dialed Ben Irvington's house and Amy said distracted, "Ben's at the hospital. Everyone and his uncle's sick. I'm terrified Benjy will get this bug, though Ben says it doesn't hit babies. . . . What's wrong with you?"

"Jeremy——"

"I'll get a message to Ben and have him call you. Take it easy. I know you won't, but I'll say it anyway. I get it from Ben."

Katie brushed her hair, washed her face, cleaned her teeth

and got into the bed at an unreasonably early hour. Then she called Olive.

"Jeremy's sick . . ." she began.

"Who isn't?" said Olive, sounding distraught. "The twins are down. They're dreadful patients, screaming bloody murder when they aren't throwing up. I called Ben Irvington and he sent over some medicine; says they'll be okay in a couple of days. Meantime I'll go nuts. I can't afford to catch this until they're all right, and I guess not even then. Frank's flat out in some motel somewhere. He's had a doctor, but wants me to leap into the car and come immediately. He said I could farm the twins out. When I told him they were both sick, he said, 'Oh my God!' and hung up."

"Olive, I'm so sorry."

"You and me both. But I can't help you, Katie. I have my hands full."

Katie opened the door then and tried to read; she didn't dare to turn on the radio. Now and then she crept to Jeremy's door and he seemed to be half asleep, half awake, muttering to himself, turning his head back and forth on the pillow.

That earlier little stab of apprehension was now a sharp and wounding dagger.

When Ben called, he sounded dead tired. He asked a few questions, listened to the answers and said, "I've some pretty sick people."

"Mary Hawkes?"

"One of the sickest. Don't tell Jeremy. I'll have medicine sent over, with directions. Follow them. See that he takes it, even if you have to wake him up every four hours. If he seems worse, call me here or at home. I'll come by in the morning anyway to see him and the Elder twins. Take it easy."

It seemed an eternity until the medicine arrived and the man driving the pharmacy car said, "From Doc Irvington." He looked half dead and Katie asked, "Can I fix you some coffee?"

"Thanks. No time. I'll be up half the night. This thing hit like a hurricane except no warning. It started maybe four days ago, here and there."

Katie looked at the directions, plodded upstairs, woke her husband, and said before he could speak, "Take this. . . . Ben sent it over. You're to have it every four hours."

"I told you not to call him," said Jeremy. "I'll be fine. Just a cold or something."

"Ben said take it and no nonsense."

"I won't keep it down."

"Don't make up your mind," said Katie.

"How does he know I'm not allergic to it?" he asked crossly. "It's probably one of those damned antibiotics."

"He doesn't know. And don't make up your mind to that either."

"I can't stand bossy women."

"Pity," said Katie.

Back to bed, up in four hours, and so on through the night.

When Katie woke, early, Jeremy was sleeping quietly and she put on a robe, went downstairs and made coffee. She thought, looking into the cup as if it contained tea leaves: I wonder why people get married? She remembered an older friend long ago who had gone off, in the hunting season, to a cabin in the woods, for her honeymoon. Her husband came down with pneumonia. She'd said to Katie and Susy Norton on her return, "Much as I love Lem all I could think of was: Why did I marry him? Why hadn't I left well enough alone? Smack in the middle of the woods, no telephone. It was ghastly."

"Count your blessings," young Mrs. Palmer told herself severely. No woods, a phone, and Ben coming soon.

He came after what seemed a couple of weeks. He looked as if he hadn't slept, but otherwise as reassuring and normal as ever. He said, "Gimme a cup, will you? That hospital brew is double hog wash. How is Jeremy?"

"He was asleep when I came down. He seems quieter."

"Good. What's his temperature?"

"I was afraid to wake him"—she hesitated and went on—"I took it during the night, but half the time I can't read the thermometer—I'm sorry, Ben."

"Well, learn," said Ben promptly and thrust his hands through his red hair until it stood on end.

Katie found herself laughing. "You look spooky," she said.

"I feel spooky. I sent my old man home; had to. I threatened to get his wife, my devoted mother, to come over. He worked half the night. This virus hits old people hard; we've lost a couple. Mary's better, but she's not old, of course." He yawned. "Sit still. I'll go upstairs."

When he came back, he found Katie asleep, her bright head on her forearm on the kitchen table.

"Hey," he said and touched her gently.

She came awake, sat up and shook her head. Her hair flew around her face. She said, "I wouldn't make a very good nurse, would I?"

"One of the worst and prettiest," he answered, smiling. "Here are written instructions. In your state you'd never remember verbal ones. Stick with them, no matter what. He's better. I think by, tomorrow his temperature will be subnormal. He'll feel like hell. His disposition will suffer. Get used to it, Katie. You'll be married for another half century or more. Men are notoriously bad patients. Doctors are worse. Amy's learned that."

"You're such a comfort," murmured Katie, pulling her warm robe about her, conscious of bare feet in bedroom slippers.

Ben said, "Do what you can for him, but don't smother him with wild embraces. I have more than I can handle now!"

She went with him to the door, and he said, "I've given him a shot. I think he'll sleep after a while. When he's able to eat—oh well, I wrote it all out. Call me this afternoon, or before if you think it necessary."

He went off with the bulky black bag, bareheaded in the bitter weather, tall, and seemingly invincible.

Jeremy was better the next morning; and his disposition was like sandpaper. Olive reported that the twins were recovering and raising hell and Frank had telephoned that he supposed he'd live. Beth called. Katie ran up and down stairs until her pretty legs ached; also her feet. Jeremy was as changeable as April—a month which seemed light years away. He wanted his pillows tussled; he'd like a window opened. No, shut it. He demanded something to read. He threw the book on the floor. He turned on a transistor for the news. It made his head ache. He wished she'd go downstairs and leave him alone. After she'd done so, he rang the bell which she had provided. She could come sit with him, keeping her distance. He wanted to sleep. He thought he'd like an eggnog; no, some milk toast.

All this she reported to Ben and he said soothingly, "He's on the mend. Keep him quiet. Feed him, when he can take it —a little at a time, and often. Amuse him."

"Amuse him!" Katie cried.

"Don't scream," said Ben reprovingly. "Yes, amuse him. Jeremy bores easily."

Cam telephoned. He said, "I understand my virus, or one

like it, is taking over the village inhabitants. Jeremy among them. Beth called me. How is he?"

"Better according to Ben. Cam, he's terrible."

"Then he's better all right," said Cam.

"I guess so. It's sort of wearing," she said. "Nothing pleases him."

"Sure, not even you," he agreed.

"Everyone all right at your place?"

"Our Mr. Jackson has the bug, and our Mrs. Latimer is looking after him. Otherwise, I'd send her over to give you a little respite."

"She might catch it, Cam."

"No virus would dare approach Polly," said Cam. "I'm a good nurse. I'll come. I can cook, I can bathe fevered bodies, I can hold heads. You'd be surprised at my many gifts. See you, honey." And he hung up.

Cam, of all people, thought Katie, incredulous. And Beth had called him, she thought further.

Cam came, read Ben's instructions and said approvingly, "Couldn't be more sensible. I'll take over. You go out and walk a while."

"Walk!"

"Yes. It's done from the brain, you know. Impulses as Jeremy would say. Elementary. Bundle up, get some fresh air, out of this so-called house."

"But——"

"Don't argue; also don't fall down and sprain another ankle. I'll have my hands full with that man you're living with. Move it, Katie, and that's an order."

As she went to the hall closet to pull out boots and other articles of clothing, she heard Cam's friendly greeting at Jeremy's door.

"So you got caught with your resistance down, you scholarly bastard. . . . How'd you like a bed bath?"

Jeremy barked back, but Katie was fleeing into the open air. It was very cold, but it felt good. She thought: What next? And then: With Cam around I can get back to the office.

18

✳✳✳✳ For the next three days Cameron Ross came and went often like a tornado, and at other times, a zephyr. He shouted, bullied and coaxed. He sent Katie back to the office. "You disturb the patient," he told her. He arrived at Baker Street after breakfast bearing casseroles and delicacies whipped up by Mrs. Latimer whose patient was showing symptoms of recovery. Jeremy was bathed, shaved, fed and medicated, also practically bludgeoned into resting, and then helped into a chair, a comfortable one that Cam carried from the study. "This thing in your guest room," he told Katie, "would send a man back to bed with a broken neck. How about that hassock from the living room, too?"

Ben came by to check on Jeremy, and also the Elder twins and listened to Cam with considerable respect.

"Sure you weren't in the Medical Corps?" he inquired.

"No sir. They armed me to the teeth."

"Then how come these skills?"

Cam grinned. "I've been in a lot of odd situations during

which I've had to look after drunks, hysterics—both male and female—accidents, camping trips," he explained vaguely, "as well as in penthouses or summer resorts. I've sent Katie back to the office. She's useless around here. It's all right at night, of course, as he sleeps. And she can make coffee, after a fashion. . . . What's wrong with her, Doc?"

"Katie?" Ben said. "She drove herself into a sort of nervous exhaustion." He smiled at Cam. "But the ankle helped because she had to rest whether she wanted to or not."

Cam made his own diagnosis. "Frustration," he decided. "Most people suffer from it, except me, of course."

"Why don't you?" Ben asked curiously. He and Cam were good, if recent, friends.

"I don't permit it. If I fail somewhere, I succeed somewhere else; if I lose something—money or a woman for instance—I find another dollar and another girl."

"Someday that horse you ride may not take the fence."

"So what? He throws me and breaks his leg or mine or both. . . . Shoot the horse, get yourself another, find a good orthopedic man and after a while throw away the crutches. . . . That's Jeremy hollering," he said unnecessarily.

On the fourth evening he called Beth, went over, picked her up and brought her back to Baker Street for supper, courtesy of Mrs. Latimer, having informed Katie that a little company would do Jeremy good. Cam had been reading the Journals during Jeremy's rest periods. On this evening, he took Jeremy downstairs and to the table for the first time. "You can have a drink," he announced, "and you're to eat. Tomorrow you'll be up and won't need me, thank God."

Jeremy had lost weight, and he was not yet quite steady on his feet. "I feel like a dishrag," he complained.

Cam said, "You're going to live, and you can look after yourself now, with a slight assist from Katie. Ben says you can mind your store the first of next week, but you're to limit your hours."

"You decide. Ben decides. What am I supposed to do?"

"Shut up, listen and obey. A fair percentage of the people hit by this bug have wound up with pneumonia, and some of them went further than that and woke up dead. This thing relapses, Ben tells me."

"Mary's not back in the shop yet," Jeremy said.

"No, and she won't be for a couple of more weeks," Katie told him. "I asked Ben."

"I asked too," said Jeremy. "Thank heavens I saw most all the salesmen before I was clobbered. But I can't sit around here——"

"It's sit," Cam said, "or back to bed. Beth says the customers are trickling back; and she and the rest of your staff can manage."

Beth agreed smiling. She said, "Please don't fret, Jeremy. Everything's going along very well."

After supper, Jeremy sat in the study for a time and they talked about Charity and her Journals. Cam had already spoken to Mason. "He's interested," said Cam, "cautiously of course, being a publisher."

"The typing's about done, the editing comes next," Beth said.

"Easy does it," Cam advised. "You can't improve much on Charity's style. Quite a gal. Wish I'd known her . . . wish I'd fought in that war. Maybe I did," he added dreamily.

"You'd like to have been in every war," said Jeremy and Beth asked, "Do we have to talk about wars?"

"You've been working on a book about one," Cam reminded her.

"Yes, but it's so far away."

"Revolutions are never far away. There's one going on

somewhere right now. Methods change, weapons change, people don't. He leaned over, kissed Beth's cheek. Then Katie said, "Cheer up, girl. Everything will return to what's known as normal, at least in this instance."

It did. Emily Warner came back from her cruise; business picked up; it had no choice once Emily was in her office. Jeremy went back to the bookshop for lengthening periods of time, and eventually Mary Hawkes did too. Customers returned from their sickbeds or those of others, Rosie Niles invited Jeremy and Katie and the Bankses for dinner, and Linda reported that she felt as good as new. Susan and her husband finally came home, their Hawaiian trip having extended itself to Hong Kong and Japan.

Jeremy found a small, valuable, very scarce pamphlet, by Florence Nightingale, at a rare edition bookseller's in Boston and sent it to Cam, who thanked him profanely over the telephone and stated that he was off to Chicago tomorrow and that he thought that Polly Latimer—"She's outside," he said, "bossing Mr. Jackson"—had found herself a steady follower.

"I don't believe it."

"Ever since she took care of him with the pip, she's been acting as if someone had given her a large, snappy, but interesting dog. She'll train him."

"How will that affect you?" Jeremy asked, laughing. He looked up at Beth as she passed his desk and said, "It's Cam."

"Who's that? . . . Beth? Give her my love and tell her not to forget our date tonight. . . . Affect me? Oh, Polly—favorably. The apartment's big enough for two. I'll give her away and throw a party."

Jeremy went home and reported to Katie, who exclaimed, "That would be wonderful. . . . What's wrong, Jeremy?"

"Nothing, except Beth seems to be seeing a lot of Cam."

"What of it? She'd make him a very good wife."

"You've heard him say he has no intention of remarrying."

"He could change his mind."

"He's my closest friend," said Jeremy, "but Beth?" He shook his head. "She's not his type."

"Who is?"

"I dunno. Sybil was once, I suppose. As for the others, they came in all shapes, sizes, and personalities. I don't like it."

Katie sparked suddenly. "Do you want to keep her a grieving war widow for the rest of her life? Don't be an idiot. She's young. She has a right to a new deal and she's too level-headed to expect the sort of lovely, brief romantic marriage she's had."

"I don't like it," he repeated stubbornly.

The spark flamed. Katie said, "Maybe you're jealous. Maybe you want to keep her in the shop, as an extra added attraction, as well as your collaborator."

Jeremy rose. He towered. He said, "You're talking like a damned fool."

"Okay," said Katie, "and you're acting like one. So from now on you can just collaborate, or whatever you call it, with Beth in the shop or at her house. I'm fed up with creeping around my own with you and Beth in the study—hearing you talk and laugh from a distance. Or keep quiet, except for the typewriters, which is worse," she decided forlornly.

Jeremy looked stunned. He said, "But that's sheer nonsense. Katie, do you think I'm in love with her?"

"Yes . . . No . . . or not yet, anyway. But I suppose the honeymoon's over, for us, I mean. And there's Beth. Propinquity," Katie said, shaking. "You're with her eight hours a day in that bloody shop and a good many evenings here and then Cam comes along and that infuriates you."

"Go on," he said stonily.

"Cam's a challenge," Katie said wildly, "so you're practicing the dog-in-the-manger bit."

"You're being absurd."

"You know, of course, that you have nothing to offer her," Katie informed him, warming up. . . . "Why you're not even *divorced*!"

Jeremy laughed then. He thought: She's such an idiot, I love her so much, but I could take her across my knee . . .

"Katie, darling," he said.

"Don't darling me," she ordered, "and don't pick me up and carry me to bed either. I'm not in the mood for reconciliation lovemaking. I won't collaborate," she pledged firmly.

"I thought you liked Beth," he said, trying not to laugh again.

"I do, but I'm not blind or deaf or stupid. Anyway, none of this is Beth's fault. She can't help looking the way she does. It's your doing——"

"I thought you loved me," he said soberly.

"I do. I wish I didn't. And anyway that doesn't alter anything."

"What do you want me to do? Fire Beth and quit work on the Journals?"

"Yes . . . No . . . I don't know what I want you to do—except not interfere between her and Cam."

He said, "I told you I felt responsible for her."

"Why? You can just stop that," said Katie. "She's a grown woman. If she wants Cam and he doesn't want her, that's their business. And you can't deny that you find her attractive."

"I'm not blind either," said Jeremy, "and most men would. . . . Come here, before I slap you."

"Don't you dare lay a hand on me."

But he hauled her out of the corner of the couch and held her. He smoothed her hair back, and smiled a little.

"And don't try to exercise your well-known charm on me either," she said, struggling.

"I love you, Katie. I'm fond of Beth and fond of Cam. I just don't want to see her hurt."

"If she's in love with Cam," said Katie, "she's asking for it maybe. Then she can cry on your shoulder."

"Katie, shut up."

For a short time she did, but later, in bed, she was back on the subject. "Like I've said before——"

"As you've said before," Jeremy corrected.

"Very well," said Katie. "My husband, the purist. *As* I've said before, 'A roll in the hay doesn't solve problems.' "

"No," he agreed, somewhat to her astonishment, "but it's a pleasant interlude."

"Will you promise me something, Jeremy?"

"Not without knowing what it is."

"Keep your hands off——"

"Beth?"

"Off the situation, and, yes, her too. As far as Cam's concerned, if he knew how you felt about this, he'd beat you to a pulp and don't tell me he couldn't."

"He knows how I feel. I've told him and I'm still intact."

"What did he say?" Katie asked.

"Told me to mind my own business, and that the Knights of the Round Table were no longer relevant. He was very much amused."

"He didn't offer to knock your block off?"

"He couldn't. He was nursing me like a brother. It isn't cricket to cream your patient."

Katie said, "Well, who are you to stand in Beth's way? All

that money, Mrs. Latimer, Mr. Jackson and a swimming pool. Besides Cam wouldn't listen to you seriously."

"Who does?" inquired her husband. "For God's sake, go to sleep."

19

✳✳✳✳ Months, in common with seasons and human beings, are capricious in the extreme. February bestowed a Valentine upon Little Oxford in the melting sunny shape of a thaw. "Early spring," said some people happily and the women, young and old of the station wagon set, got out their wool shorts and even appeared in them on Colonial Way and other streets, long hair tossing, knees turning indigo. After which February sulked behind large dark clouds and snowed as fitfully as an aged person naps. When it didn't snow, it was savagely cold, thermometers plunged to zero and furnaces, also capricious, went on strike and the repair men toiled through many nights. The fire department was busy. Now and again branches crashed, and the power went off. So people said sadly, "A late spring."

But on clear nights the sunsets were pure gold, surrounded by a pale green sea, rosy clouds floating by like ships.

Beth and Jeremy had finished the first typing, and the Journals were ready for editing, which Jeremy had undertaken. Beth, he said, would retype when he'd finished. In effect, a compromise, as is most of living, Katie reflected.

Cam was in and out of Little Oxford; and in March Ronnie came for her pre-Easter vacation. The ice in ponds and lakes was still solid and she together with Mrs. Latimer and Mr. Jackson went skating. Also Ronnie was learning to cook, Mrs. Latimer having insisted. "You won't always have your dad," she told her, "and maybe he won't always have a great deal of money; you could marry a poor young man."

"I," said Ronnie, with dignity, "am not nuts."

"That's as may be, but the way the world's heading—what with wars, natural disasters, unnatural disasters and taxes, to say nothing of unemployment—a girl, even one as young as you, should be prepared."

Ronnie took a burning interest in everything. When able to get transportation, she popped into the book store and stayed for hours, observing customers and clerks. Some customers actually brought small children, and others dogs. She sat on Jeremy's desk until he threw her out. She listened to salesmen earnestly selling; she followed Beth around and decided there was more to selling a book than just writing one. She also came calling on Katie at the agency. Mrs. Warner took a fancy to her. She said, "She has a head on her shoulders. I think she'll probably land in Government, although one doesn't always follow the other."

Katie took Ronnie out on several trips, when she was certain that the prospective client didn't hate children. And Ronnie twice discovered a flaw in a prospective rental. Once, she proclaimed, crawling under a sink, "this leaks." And the next time, down in the cellar, she cried triumphantly, "Termites!"

This did not endear her to the people showing their houses at a very stiff seasonal rental for the coming summer, but

Katie was grateful. She should have seen the defects herself.

Ronnie also spent time in a record shop where one was permitted to play records in a private booth. Before she left Little Oxford, Jeremy, Katie and Beth Nelson dined at Cam's and Ronnie came to dinner with the Palmers alone.

"Much as I love her," said Cam over the telephone, "this has been a very long week. I even went to the city twice when I didn't have to and the indispensable Mrs. Latimer is worn out, between her cautious love life and my insane offspring. Will you take her for the evening? I'll drop her off and pick her up." He added, "I have a date."

Ronnie came, smartly attired, and bearing a gift, an album. She said, presenting it to Katie, "David Cassidy. I'm sure Jeremy won't be interested, but even middle-aged women —not that you're really middle-aged—I just mean people over, maybe, eighteen like Dave. You can play it when Jeremy isn't around. How about after supper?"

"He'll be around, Ronnie. But he's working."

Jeremy emerged into the hall and said, "I could spare a little while to sit in." He put his arm around Ronnie's shoulders, "Looks as if I'd been supplanted," he told her.

"What's that?"

"You've thrown me over," Jeremy deduced.

"Well, not exactly," she said as Katie marched her into the study for ginger ale and Jeremy concocted something stronger for his wife and himself. "Of course David's an older man, too," she explained sighing. And then brightened, "There's a boy in the next apartment," she began, "he's thirteen . . ."

They had hamburgers and French fries, having consulted their guest beforehand. "Vegetables," Ronnie said, "don't send me, but I have to eat them. When I'm older, I'll eat only what I want. I'll be thinner then," she promised.

Ice cream, however, was acceptable.

After supper they played the album. "He turns me on," said Ronnie, "but I'm not really overboard, and I just hate being called a teeny bopper. Did you know he has green eyes?"

They hadn't known until then.

Afterward Katie took her into the living room and said firmly, "Jeremy has to work."

"Natch. So now it's talk time?"

"What do you want to talk about?"

"Beth, for openers," replied Ronnie, who watched a lot of television.

"What about her?"

"Don't pretend. Everyone knows Dad is crazy about her."

"They're good friends," conceded Katie.

Ronnie raised her eyebrows and shrugged, and Katie thought: I bet her mother does that.

"That's what Mrs. Latimer said," Ronnie told her. "She also said children should be seen and not heard. She's a real dropout."

"From what?" Katie asked, laughing. Ronnie was so adult and so childish and so earnest.

"From like it is now. She belongs back in—who was that queen who always said, 'We are not amused'?"

"Queen Victoria."

"That's her," said Ronnie with a regrettable lack of syntax. "Anyway, Dad's had thousands of good friends. I liked a few; some were pretty silly or dumb, and a few I hated. Creeps. Men," said Ronnie, "have a rough time—some woman always after them. But Beth's all right, I think. She's square, of course, but I don't hold it against her. And she doesn't try to treat me as if I were six, or a brat. She doesn't try to mother me either. Most of Dad's girlfriends I've met —he'd bring them to school or the penthouse or take me out to lunch with them—most of them did one thing or the other, and if there's anything I don't need it's a mother. I've got one," said Ronnie, concluding, "and one's all I can handle."

"Ronnie, you shoudn't be discussing——"

"Rats," said Ronnie. "You're Dad's friend, aren't you?"

"Of course, but——"

"And Beth's."

"Why, yes," Katie admitted.

"And mine. I thought you were my friend."

"I am," Katie said vigorously.

"Then what's the harm? I'm telling you because I think this time he's serious and I'm all for it—or ninety-five percent. No one's really a hundred percent for *anything*," said Ronnie.

Katie's curiosity conquered her caution. She asked, "All right. Why?"

"She's great to look at," said Ronnie. "I hope I can have a figure like that someday, but I don't suppose I ever will. She's fun to be around. She never shouts; she doesn't make scenes——"

"Well, in the circumstances I doubt she would——"

"Are you kidding?" asked Ronnie. "I've been in on lots of scenes. My mother's a scene maker. Boy can she ever make scenes! But, of course, she's my responsibility. Beth's quiet and she's sensible and I honestly don't think the money matters too much; of course, it could be a figure—I don't mean that, exactly, do I?"

"I think you mean, factor."

"Right on. She'd be dumb if it weren't. But I think she's in love with him."

Katie said hastily, "Honestly, Ronnie, I'd so much rather not have you talking behind your father's and Beth's back——"

"I'm not, because I've told him, too, just the other night. Don't you want to know what he said?"

"No," said Katie, lying in her teeth.

"Sure, you do. All he said was, 'I should be so lucky.' I think she's keeping him guessing, but maybe I'm wrong; maybe she wouldn't have him; all that traveling and parties and people," said Ronnie. "Or maybe it's me."

"I'm sure it's not, dear."

"And I talked to Beth too. She took me to the ice-cream parlor on her lunch hour Wednesday. She wasn't mad or anything. All she said was she was glad I liked her. End of talk time. But you can tell Jeremy," Ronnie added kindly, "I still love him a lot, even though I have other interests now."

Cam called for his daughter about ten. He said, "Sorry to be late. Beth and I had dinner over the county line. Where's Jeremy?"

"Still working."

"And what have you two young women been talking about? Did Ronnie tell you she hears that long hair is going out?"

"We didn't get around to it," Ronnie said.

"We were just talking," she added in answer to his inquiry. "You know how it is."

"I do not," he told her gravely, "thank heaven." He put his arm around his child and asked, "Any complaints?"

"Nope. Except I have to go back to that dumb school. It's a drag."

"One day you won't have to. . . . Thanks, Katie. Tell Jeremy I hope he'll soon be through with the editing job."

Jeremy came in saying, "I'm sorry, but it's almost over. It's been most rewarding. But I have trouble switching back to this century."

"Sometimes," remarked Katie, "you don't entirely succeed."

After the Bentley had purred away into the frosty night, Katie said, "I've something to tell you. Ronnie said I might."

"Well, good for her. I'd hate to think you two kept secrets from me."

They were upstairs now and Katie continued, watching him in the mirror, "She was talking about her father and Beth."

Jeremy dropped a shoe. "So?" he inquired.

"Nothing, except she approves. She hopes they'll get married. She's told Beth so and also Cam."

"And what did they say?"

"Not very much. Cam said he should be so lucky—and if you say 'as,' I'll scream—and Beth said she was glad that Ronnie liked her."

"Well," said Jeremy, "all he needs now is Mrs. Latimer's —and maybe Mr. Jackson's—approval. Sybil doesn't count, nor does Cam's brother and his family. Incidentally his father has always disliked Sybil and has hoped ever since the divorce that Cam would find a fine capable woman, pretty enough to be his hostess, smart enough to slow him down. He's said it to me, which is how I know."

"Please drop the other shoe, darling."

Jeremy obliged. He said, "But if he has your approval and Ronnie's, he's halfway to the church or whatever."

"He doesn't have Beth's, or not yet, apparently. Have you taken it upon yourself to talk to her?"

"A couple of times," he admitted uneasily.

"For a clever man, you are incredibly stupid, or maybe for a grown man, adolescent," Katie commented, brushing her hair.

"Maybe," he admitted. He padded across the room to lean down and kiss her. "I seem to be fighting a losing battle."

"One more windmill to cross," said Katie absurdly, "and it isn't your battle. As Cam said, Sir Galahad, or whoever, isn't relevant. And Cam's no fire-breathing dragon, Jeremy."

"I simply want everyone to be happy—Beth—and Cam—as happy as I am, most of the time."

"I'll overlook that last remark. Then why don't you give up and let them make the discovery? Whether they're happy or not isn't up to you. There's no use trying to thicken the plot."

"You're full of strange misplaced quotations and clichés," Jeremy said, shaking his head.

"You married me for better or worse. . . . By the way, there's land for sale, out beyond the Irvington house—or there will be, next month. Two acres, woods, a little brook. You couldn't walk to town—well I suppose you could, but it might be difficult in winter. Shall we look at it? Emily will give us first chance. It's an exclusive with her—us."

"As has often been said," Jeremy remarked, "this is so sudden."

"Darling, it would be a marvelous investment. We don't have to build right away. But we'd have it to build on when we're ready. The market's going to go up, not down. We can wait; if we don't build, we can resell profitably. Say you'll look at it," she urged.

He said after a moment, "All right. God defend us against aggressive real estate agents, especially females. But there's no harm in looking," he decided, "if we can afford it."

"We can. I've squirreled quite a lot away. I've had pretty good luck since we were married and as you insist upon keeping me—rent, food, insurance—I'm fairly well off, so we can go into it fifty-fifty. Like—as," she added hastily—"a marriage should be."

"We'll see," said Jeremy. "Get to bed, will you?" He got in beside her and switched off the light. "Cam's going to make an appointment for me to see Mason," he added, and then, "Did you say two acres?"

20

✳✳✳✳ March had been normal—wild, wet, windy, with snow showers and sudden warm spells. Katie was busy; when her car decided to take a vacation in the shop, Emily offered hers. "I'm getting too old," she complained, "to crash over country roads, climb stairs, coax, and listen. When I retire, how about taking over? You're the youngest and most able and ambitious."

Katie laughed, "Your retirement is a long way off," she predicted.

"Old firehorse?" asked Emily. "Well, I suppose so. But Bing Irvington keeps saying, 'Slow up.' He's been saying it for years and I have, as you may have noticed."

"But I couldn't afford it," Katie told her.

"We'll see. It won't be tomorrow or next week. Meantime how about the Hanbury house?"

Construction burgeoned, and people came from the city, and from distances to look, inquire, and haggle. They came in all kinds of weather, tramping through mud, ice patches and puddles. Some were executives whose companies were moving them and their families; others, widows, widowers, or elderly couples, looking for condominiums; still others, young people intent upon acquiring "a modest little place in the country" near good schools. Katie would come home, tired to her little bones and Jeremy would take her out to dinner or preside in the kitchen. But he was occasionally in the city, and Beth went with him a time or two for conferences with Mr. Mason and others in the publishing firm. The Journals had been accepted, but they needed more editorial work. One of the editorial staff was taking over.

April came in sweet and cold as an ice-cream cone, and also sloppy. Easter arriving early in that month, the seasonal bunny whipped up a considerable snow fall, snarling traffic, delaying planes. The snow stayed only briefly on the ground, but during it church congregations thinned out, women with new Easter finery—those few who bothered—stayed home or went out and caught cold. April, too, was normal.

Jeremy and Katie went to inspect the two acres near the edge of town—really country. "There's so little land left," Katie reminded him anxiously as they walked about in boots and heavy windbreakers. The small brook, ice-rimmed but full, laughed at them as they stood beside it. There were a great many trees, all neglected—elms, dogwood, maples, hickory, oaks—and tangles of bushes.

"Take a lot of clearing," Jeremy said, "and at the price asked, it doesn't seem feasible."

"But we wouldn't clear, at least not much, unless we decide to build. And trees are valuable, we'd leave plenty. The price isn't exorbitant, Jeremy."

"No town water," Jermy objected, "or sewage."

"This piece has never been built on," Katie told him, "and if we build we can put in a septic tank and a good artesian well."

"Who owns this?"

"It's part of the Treslow estate. The original place had eighty acres. The house is owned by a grandson, he's sold off fifty acres. These are the last lots left. The zoning is just two acres in this area; the land value will increase like crazy."

"Taxes?"

She told him. He shook his head.

"Mortgage?"

"None."

"If we build," he said, "plus septic tank, well, clearing and a second car—the cost will be astronomical."

"When we do, if we do. Meantime, as I've said, it's an investment. Land's better than stocks and bonds. We can hold it a year, maybe two, until we decide."

"I'll have to go to the bank," he said gloomily.

"What's so terrible about that? Your credit's better than good; and you're not exactly penniless. When you are," she said, looking up at him, "we can sell and maybe be rich."

"Who else has brought Treslow property?"

"People who have built on three, four, even six acres. I'll show you the houses. No developments. And, of course, people like Mrs. Warner who haven't built."

"Emily!"

"She's been buying land for some time, every time there's a recession. She doesn't buy for the agency, but for herself."

"Well I'll be damned!" said Jeremy. "Though I really don't know why. Well, let's go home and think it over."

So they went home that Sunday, presumably to think, and Jeremy said over a drink, "Okay. You're used to bargaining, so I'll bargain."

"What's your proposition?" Katie asked warily.

"We'll buy, and at the end of a year, if you consent to an increase in the population, we'll build. No sense in owning property without progeny."

"That's sneaky," Katie said hotly, "and we'd lose my income."

"Oh," he told her carelessly, "you can still work awhile in the office, and even out of it. And go back after a reasonable length of time."

After a while she said slowly, "Mrs. Warner would like me to take on the agency after she retires. It's something to consider. She'd retain an interest, of course, and God knows what she'd ask for the business. Also, if you feel you have to borrow to buy the land, what about the cost of building and starting a family?"

"Why do you think I've been hanging on to the money left after I came here and bought out the bookshop? I hung on for the future—land, houses. I've done all right on Cam's advice. We can swing it, with caution and a little luck. As for yourself, you can take a leave of absence for a while, we'll find someone to look after the offspring. . . . Believe me, Katie, Emily isn't ready to retire. When she does, you can cope."

"I don't like to bargain with you."

"Sleep on it. Take a week, take two."

"I can't. Either we buy that land within a few days or Mrs. Warner will show it to our clients. Maybe I'll have to show it," she added mournfully, "and that would kill me."

"I doubt it. Sleep on it, as I said, and report to me at breakfast."

"But it isn't fair. Bargaining!"

"You want something, I want something; bargaining is as much a part of marriage as it is of any business. Take it or leave it. Finish your drink and I'll take you to the Inn for dinner. And no shop talk of any kind. Cabbages and kings, the weather—and have you gone back to your mid-child-hood? I heard you playing the Cassidy records this morning. I'll stick with Sinatra. And we'll talk about going up to see Susy and Roger in a few weeks, and about Charity, my next-to-favorite woman."

"Wait a minute," said Katie. "You're not bargaining with me; you're trying to bribe me!"

"Negative. A bargain is a transaction usually arrived at by haggling on both sides. . . . I state a price; you make me an offer; eventually I come down a little, and you go up the same amount. Also a bargain is something you pay less for than you expected to—the language is full of multiple definitions. But a bribe is offered in the hope of corrupting the prospective taker."

"You make me tired," said Katie, yawning extravagantly.

"Sorry about that. Comes of reading dictionaries—there were so many of them around. Retentive memory, too. Almost total recall."

"What color was I wearing when you met me?"

"Something pale gold, flecked with rainbow sequins."

"In an *office?*"

"My memory also retains emotional reactions. As a matter of fact, it was brown—a color which doesn't become you. . . . Go fix your face."

She went upstairs muttering to herself. Brown? I never wear brown . . . well—there was that old but still useful rag mother gave me in a fit of absentmindedness.

When they'd returned from the Inn where, at a corner table, they had discussed a number of things and opinions unrelated to wooded lots or pregnancies, Katie went up-stairs, leaving Jeremy to ponder an editorial suggestion relating to the Journals. Then he, too, retired and about three the next morning Katie shook him awake.

"What's wrong?" he demanded. "Who . . . oh, Katie, I was having a superb dream."

"What about?"

"Concord, Massachusetts. There was a phantom horse, galloping through it."

"That was another silversmith, name of Revere."

"Why did you wake me? Did you hear something?" He switched on the light. There had been prowlers in the area, so now he was wide awake.

But Katie said, "Don't bother. I didn't hear anything except you, sort of whooping and hollering in a whisper. That's one reason why I woke you. I've been like an owl for hours."

"What other reason?" he inquired.

"Your proposition. I'll take it. Go back to sleep. See if you can get away from the shop about ten, and meet me at the agency. Good night. Turn off the light. You look stunned."

"So I am."

"Too easy?" she inquired. "I'm stunned, too. How I could give up——"

"You gave in," Jeremy said. He kissed her and switched off the lamp, saying, "We'll go for broke."

"Of course," Katie agreed. "It costs the earth to buy property which is suitable; but have you considered what it costs to be parents? Hospital, nurses—I love nurses—someone helpful about the house, eventually a Nanny type. Then there's school, clothing, teeth straightening, shots, diseases, college."

"Keep quiet, I'm asleep," said Jeremy.

On the following day Katie marched into the office and asked immediately if she could consult Mrs. Warner.

"Well?" asked Emily, regarding her, "you look most peculiar. Like one of those comedy-tragedy masks, half smiling, half weeping."

"We'll buy the property," Katie told her, "so Jeremy is coming in at ten to discuss it with you."

Emily's black eyes gleamed. "You'll never regret it, Katie. It's a bargain," she said.

Katie shuddered. "Don't mention bargaining or bribes, please."

"What are you talking about?"

"Jeremy's made a bargain with me, but I think it's a bribe. He explained the difference—which I don't buy."

"He would. . . . What was it, exactly?"

Katie told her and Emily was silent for a moment, tapping a pencil on the desk. Then, "Cheer up. You could, of course, cheat a little," she suggested.

"Cheat?"

"Well, *don't* stop doing whatever it is you are doing," Emily suggested delicately. "A lot of women can't have children," she explained kindly, "sometimes never, sometimes for years."

"Jeremy," Katie answered, "is not stupid. He'd have me in Ben's office in no time—given a few months in which he'd decide whether I were cheating or not. Besides," she added, "I wouldn't."

"I daresay."

"But I want to go on working," Katie told her.

"I know, and you shall. It will be inconvenient for me, also for you, and expensive for you and Jeremy, but we'll work it out. I'm not losing my best agent to pablum and diapers or whatever it is contemporary babies demand. Are you supposed to get pregnant as soon as the papers are signed?"

"No. He said in a year if I consented to an increase in the population."

"You're putting me on."

"His exact words. Then we'd build. I feel disloyal," Katie admitted, "but I have to talk to someone and you're the only person I know who'd understand—at least, about how I feel about working."

Emily sighed. She said, "My advice—and you certainly needn't follow it—is don't wait a year. Wait, say, until the end of summer. Business will be slower after the autumn months; then comes winter. Jeremy will be delighted. You can start the house as well as the baby, and you'll have a place to move into when he or she arrives. I wonder which?"

"Ask Jeremy," Katie suggested. "He knows everything. He'll look in a dictionary."

"A what? . . . Never mind. Just try to time things if possible."

"With my luck," said Katie, "it will be the elephant's child."

"Katie, are you sure you aren't running a temperature?"

"I'm not running anything. I read Kipling when I was young—*Jungle Tales* I think. But I wasn't referring to Mr. K. I was thinking I'll probably carry a baby however long the elephant carries hers. I think, maybe, it's two years," she said and Emily put her hands over her face and laughed hard enough for Flo, in the reception room, to hear her and inquire of empty space: "Has she lost her mind, or sold the Gannon place?" Which was a rhetorical but apt question, as everyone in the agency referred to that great Victorian structure as a white elephant.

21

✳✳✳✳ That evening Katie thought: Emily's a female computer. According to her, this whole deal can be neatly packaged. Spring and summer, I'm to work like mad. Come autumn, I can still be useful though pregnant; and the house will be taking shape. Therefore by spring, complete with infant, Jeremy and I leave Baker Street. But computers are subject to human error.

"What are you smiling over?" Jeremy inquired.

"I was thinking of Emily, our almost human computer."

"We got along fine," Jeremy reminded her. "She even blew us to lunch."

"Of course. She likes you; she's always liked you, but now more so. When you wouldn't buy what is now Cam's house, she downgraded you. Now she has you in her pocket."

"Pocketbook."

"Well, yes. She thinks you're brilliant. Incidentally she recommended three architects before I left the office. I know 'em all. . . . The best and incidentally the least expensive, is also the youngest. You've met him, I'm sure. Lee Osborne. He's in the firm of Harmon and Sanford. They're years older."

"Of course, I know Lee," said her husband. "He's a very nice guy and a good customer, too. Every time we get in another book on Greece I have to call him. He's hooked on Greece. Whenever he has a vacation, he flies over and spends his time in little villages on one or the other of the islands. Says he's a frustrated archeologist at heart."

"I don't think he's married," Katie said idly.

"Naturally not. What woman, in her right mind, would marry someone who departs whenever possible for isolated places, without modern conveniences? But, to return to Emily, she seems to be rushing our fences. The papers aren't even signed and she talks of architects. What about builders?" ·

"She hasn't gotten around to them yet."

The telephone scolded, Jeremy answered it. "It's Amy," he reported. "Wants to talk to you."

"Hi," said Katie, into the transmitter.

"Did I get you out of the kitchen?"

"No, but I'm always happy when someone does."

"My heart bleeds for Jeremy. . . . Look, Ben's upstate at a medical meeting. He'll be gone until tomorrow. Grandma Letty is certain that, left alone with Benjy, I'll either throw him out with the bath water—not that he is bathed at this hour—or burn the house down. So we're going to the Grandparents' for the night. Late dinner, too, because of Dad Bing. May I stop by, with child? He's really very good, Katie, three-quarters of the time, and Jeremy can amuse him. I want to talk to you about something before I forget it, which would be tomorrow at noon."

"Come along," Katie invited, consumed with curiosity.

"What's up?" Jeremy asked when she broke the connection.

"Who knows?" She repeated the conversation, and looked at the clock. "Probably dinner any time after eight," she decided. "Prepare yourself to entertain the baby. You may as well get used to it," she told him, "for future reference."

"I'll read books," he promised, smiling at her. "We've a big stock dealing with infancy, adolescence and right through to what to do with your senile parents."

Her heart trembled as if stroked by a feather. When Jeremy smiled like that—and he did so only during their intimate moments—his face was illuminated by tenderness.

She thought, sighing inwardly: I'm committed—still unwilling, but committed.

Amy came by presently. Jeremy went out and lifted Benjy from the car contraption, and carried him, chortling, into the house. "What am I supposed to do now?" he inquired, his arms full of sleepy, healthy humanity.

"Put him down on the floor. Here's a blanket. Wait a minute until I feel his pants. . . . Good. He'll do for now."

"And then?" asked Jeremy.

"He'll sleep, if heaven is merciful. There's a crib for him at the Irvingtons'. Grandparents think of everything. Now, just squat down and hypnotize him. I want to discuss something with your wife."

"If it's privileged, top secret or X-rated, you girls can go into the study."

"It's general public," Amy assured him, and sat down on the couch beside Katie. "Mind your manners," she told her son, who opened one eye, gurgled and closed it again. "He can creep," she said proudly, "only at the moment he's too lazy. Benjy's the finest example of his generation," she went on, "according to his parents, grandparents and great grandfather. . . . Katie, you know I used to work at Lovemay's?"

"What's that?" Katie asked, watching Jeremy. "I've forgotten if I ever knew."

"It's a publishing firm. Since the mergers, a long time ago, it has more names, but that's beside the point. It was founded by Letty's grandfather. Do you know," she added, "I never know what I'm going to call her—Letty, Mom, Grandma?—well, anyway, I worked there until I quit and came to Little Oxford to live with Elsie and Russ—you know my sister and her spouse?"

"So?" asked Katie.

"Wait a while, I'm leading up to something. I did all sorts of dog body jobs. Lovemay's was a smallish firm then. Anyway I knew a girl in the art department. Very talented," said Amy. "I didn't know her well, just at the office—but I liked her. That is, until I discovered that the man I was currently crazy about, and dating, was also dating her. Perhaps that was one reason why I quit."

"Hey," said Jeremy, "maybe Benjy and I should retire to the study."

"It's not necessary. Ben knows all about my ill-fated hangup on Bob Armitage. Anyway, I came to live here and not very long thereafter Stacy Ware married him and off they went to Chicago. He had a very successful older brother who offered him a better deal."

"In publishing?" asked Jeremy and Benjy emitted a fretful sound, feeling neglected.

"No. Do entertain your young visitor. Bob was in the Lovemay accounting department."

Katie said blankly, "What's all this leading up to——"

"Hush. Naturally I didn't keep in touch with Stacy, but I had an announcement of their wedding. By that time I had other interests, so I sent her something suitable—a cheese board, I think—and had a note thanking me. But this morning she telephoned me; I'd sent her and Bob my announcement and she must have kept the name and address, so she could find us in the book or through information."

Katie was laughing. "Naturally, you sent her an announcement," she said.

"Women!" remarked Jeremy and Benjy chuckled.

Amy looked at her. She said, "The ancestors will panic, especially Letty. She'll evision me and Benjy—not necessarily in order of importance, although actually my mother-in-law is devoted to me—dead on the roadside. So I'll make this brief. Stacy's divorced—I could have predicted it—and back in the city, free lancing. She hates it. She has, I gather, some money; I suppose a settlement from dear Bob, and possibly something from her professional parents. She wants a little house out this way, maybe someone's guest house or studio. She'd like to rent with an option to buy if it proves suitable. So she's coming out to stay with us the weekend after next. I thought you could show her around."

"I'd love to," said Katie, mentally going over the agency list, the exclusives, the multiple.

Amy rose. She said, "I was probably nuts to ask her. Ben isn't any more susceptible than the next man, but you know how the next man is!"

"She's beautiful?" inquired Katie, thinking of Beth.

"No . . . just personality . . . as I remember her she was an intense gal, sort of smoldering. Rather like Rosie Niles, in a way."

Jeremy picked up Benjy who clung to him, digging in like a koala.

"Stacy's an odd name; pretty though," Katie remarked.

"As I recall it, the name on the announcement was Anastasia, which astonished me."

Jeremy said, "Benjy looks like you and also like Ben. Your eyes—and, I think he's going to have red hair."

"If he doesn't," said Amy, touching her son's small coppery fluff, "Ben will divorce me. Okay, and thanks. I'll let you know when she comes, Katie, and if she's really ready to go house hunting."

Jeremy put her and Benjy in the car and Amy said, "It's so nice that you and Katie, Ben and I belong to the same small club."

"Which is?"

"The happily married. There isn't big membership, you know. Poor Stacy. Jeremy, please phone the in-laws and say Benjy and I are on our way. I hope Ben hasn't called—not that he's apt to before midnight. He gets wound up at these meetings and, usually, in some kind of a hassle."

Jeremy watched her drive off and returned to the house, called Letty, and sat down to think about architects. It's a step in the right direction, he told himself, even if it's a year or more away.

Katie said, after a moment, "Little Oxford has more than its share of pretty women."

"Name a few."

"Amy, Beth—she's a little more than that—and, of course, me." Then she added, "And in the other generation, Letty Irvington is fabulous; Rosie Niles, special; and of course, there's Jessica."

"Dozens more," said Jeremy promptly, "most of my favorite customers."

"I wonder if Rosie would have dinner with us? We owe her—and she really doesn't care what she eats."

"Well, thanks, seeing that I officiate deftly when we have guests."

"Steak," Katie decided. "Almost everyone likes steak."

"They'd better get weaned from it at current prices. We'll have to start too. We'll soon own property."

Katie said, "If we had a fireplace—and when we build

our house let's have at least one, also walk-in closets and lots of bookshelves—well, if we had one now, I'd say throw another log on the fire."

"In April?"

"Especially in April. . . . I'm going to call Rosie while the mood's still with me."

But Abby, who answered, reported that Mrs. Niles was away for a few days. No, she didn't know exactly when she'd be home, but she'd give her the message.

"Oh, dear," Katie said to herself.

The next day, which was Tuesday, she drove to the Banks house after delivering a client to the railroad station. She'd called first and Jessica had said, "Do come, Katie, we haven't seen you in too long. Could you make it for tea?"

She did, and they talked and Katie said, "We've bought a couple of acres—the last piece of the Treslow land."

Jessica's lovely sensitive face was alive with pleasure. "I'm so happy for you. I know you've always wanted your own place—and Jeremy too. Will you build?"

"After a while."

"It must be great fun," said Jessica. "I came to a ready-made house. I've always lived in someone else's house, including my parents'."

"We haven't discussed what it will be like, Jessica. The papers aren't signed yet. We have no immediate plans, really."

"Build it small enough for you two and big enough for a couple more," Jessica advised.

Katie's eyes widened. She said, "Jessica, you're really too much!"

"Just logical, dear."

"You sound like Jeremy. I telephoned Rosie last night, but she's away. Abby didn't know when she'd return."

"Rosie's often away."

"I know, but it worries me, this time."

"So you know about Quiet House," Jessica said.

"Yes. She told me."

"I love her dearly," said Jessica. "You will too, I think, in time."

"I do already."

"She needs that. Oh, her interest in young people—that's important, but love's even more so. She has good friends in Little Oxford who, each in his, or her own way supply it. She'll make it, Katie. I was never more sure of anything. The quiet retreats, away from here, are becoming less frequent and shorter. . . . There's Gordon."

Jessica's husband came in, had his cup of tea, and presently Katie left. She didn't understand Jessica, but she admired and respected her; also, she was growing fond of her. She thought: If I ever needed someone to talk to—besides Jeremy —I'd go to her—or Rosie."

Amy telephoned her at the office in a high gear. "Guess what?" she said.

"Your old pal, Stacy, has changed her mind," Katie deduced, resigned, "or she's gone back to her abominable snow man."

"Snow man, he ain't. He melts fast. No, the grandparents have acquired a dog."

"What's so unusual about that?" Katie inquired. "We have partnership in Lancelot, next door."

"I forgot you didn't know Tinker, Bing's dog. I knew him; he lived to be very old. After he died—Bing put him to sleep himself—Bing wouldn't replace him. Now, he says, he's acquired one for Benjy."

"What breed?"

"It's a beagle pup. Anyway, Bing says Benjy required a dog. Ben wouldn't let me have one. He decided that I knew less about dogs than I did about babies and he hadn't planned for a baby. Personally, I think he didn't want one because of Tinker. This one's named Oscar."

"Why?"

"Who knows. He's to help me bring up Benjy."

May came in on a white and rosy tide. Everything was pink and gold and sometimes Katie said spring looked like an immense soda, vanilla, raspberry. She and Jeremy went often to their property and discovered ancient apple trees, and wild beautiful dogwoods, strangled by vines, and Jeremy said, "As the days get longer I can come here and work evenings. We'll bring a picnic supper. You can help me."

"Maybe I'll just sit and watch," Katie said, and added, "You're a city boy, but I suppose you have books about what to do when a couple of acres has gone back to jungle."

"I have a great many books," Jeremy said, "and now that the Journal is on its way to fame and, I hope, fortune, I can read how to save money, beautify land, improve my health and so on."

Cam, back in Little Oxford, dropped in to the bookshop and announced, "I've problems. May I consult you privately?"

"Such as?" asked Jeremy, at his desk in the office.

"Mrs. Latimer. My Polly. She isn't getting married after all; but, she's been asked."

"So Barkis was willing?"

"By which I presume you mean Mr. Jackson. Oh certainly, in spades. But he doesn't like the apartment and she won't move into his house. He's stubborn New, she's stubborn Old, England. I had a serious talk with her about it and she told me that at their age, things were better just as they were. Exactly what she meant by that I haven't the slightest idea. It's hard to believe she's embarked upon the primrose path, but it could be———"

Jeremy laughed, "Difficult to imagine, yes. Not impossible."

"You astonish me. Have you no morals? Incidentally have you books relevant to properly conducted second marriages?"

Jeremy said slowly, "So you and Beth———"

"Keep quiet. I know you don't approve. She knows it too, but you'll come around. We'll stop by Baker Street and tell you and Katie officially, this evening. Until then, keep your big open mouth shut; shut it now, as a starter."

"But Ronnie———"

"Ronnie's going to be bridesmaid, Katie, matron of honor, and you're best man. Gordon Banks will marry us. Small reception at my little pad. But before that, Beth's resignation. Then, as it will be in June, we're off to Europe, both business and pleasure. The firm's got something cooking in Paris."

He opened the office door and went out, said, "Hi, Beth" as he passed her, and Beth smiled. "Hi," she said casually.

"Beth and Cam are stopping by," Jeremy told Katie when they were having supper.

"Good. What for?"

"I've no idea."

"I have." She left the table and went around to pat his shoulder. "Don't take it so hard," she said sympathetically.

"But suppose I was—am—right?"

"Then you'll be happy, because they're unhappy. But they won't be, you'll see," Katie told him.

Beth and Cam were married in June—"like everyone else," said Cam—and later sent postals from various large European cities and one from a small Italian village. Jeremy engaged a young pleasant woman who had been employed in a big bookshop upstate and Katie went quietly to see Ben Irvington. Then she talked to Emily Warner.

"The computer's gone haywire," she told her.

"What do you mean, computer?"

"The timing according to Emily Warner. I think I'm pregnant."

Emily rallied. "Well if you are," she said, doing mental calculations, "you've still the summer in which to be active, unless you're going to be one of those 'mornings I want to die women.'"

"I won't. I refuse to be."

"Very well. And you'll still be presentable in early autumn. After that I can use you in the office as long as you're up to it."

"Mrs. Warner," said Katie, and her mouth shook a little, "you're an angel."

"Well that's a new one," said Emily. She rose majestically and put her arm around Katie's shoulders.

"You're scared?"

Katie nodded and Emily said, "I would be, too. Maybe, I am right now. So we're both damned fools."

Katie waited for Ben to telephone. When he did, she was alone. Jeremy had gone to work. "You sure?" she asked.

"I'm sure. So's the lab. Congratulate Jeremy for me. As for you, come see me and get your orders."

"All right."

"Phone Elvira for an appointment. May I tell Amy?"

"Guess so. Yes, of course, I'm going to need her."

"You don't need Amy, grasshopper mind, scatter-brained woman. You need me—and Jeremy."

That evening Katie said furiously, "Will you stop reading those books on trees and landscaping or whatever and come here? I've something to say."

"You usually have."

"I decided that we'll have Lee Osborne for the house. Also I sold the Gannon place today. Business," said Katie, "is fantastic."

Jeremy sat down beside her, and took her hand. He said, "So you're going to reach for the brass ring, whatever happens."

"That's right. I'm a driving, nervous go-getting ambitious woman. Why not? I've realized my original and biggest ambition."

"Which was?"

"The gold ring," she answered, displaying it. "Now about the house. Southwest exposure," she said dreamily. "That's best for our bedroom."

He shook her gently. "Are you trying to tell me something, Katie?" he asked.

She kissed him and then she told him.

"Don't look as if you'd just conquered Gaul," she ordered. "I'm not ecstatic. But maybe I will be. Now, I'm scared, but I'll get over it. And I'm just as ornery as ever; perhaps I'll be more so," she said thoughtfully. "We're the same people, Jeremy, only we're going to have a house and a child. Also I suspect a tighter budget. But none of this changes us overnight. We're simply a little older and a little more married. I think maybe I'll like it, once I accept it."

"I love you," Jeremy said. "And all of Gaul is divided into three parts—physical, mental and spiritual."

"I'll buy that," said Katie gravely.